AFTER LEAVING MR MACKENZIE

Jean Rhys was born in Dominica in 1894 and came to England in her teens. After her father died she drifted into a series of jobs – chorus girl, mannequin, artist's model – and only began to write when the first of her three marriages broke up. She was living in Paris then and was encouraged by Ford Madox Ford, who wrote an enthusiastic introduction to her first book, a collection of stories called *The Left Bank*, published in 1927. This was followed by *Quartet* (1928, originally *Postures*), *After Leaving Mr Mackenzie* (1930), *Voyage in the Dark* (1934) and *Good Morning, Midnight* (1939). None of these were particularly successful, partially, perhaps, because they were decades ahead of their time in theme and tone. With the outbreak of war and subsequent failure of *Good Morning, Midnight*, her work went out of print and Jean Rhys literally dropped completely from sight. It was generally thought that she was dead. Nearly twenty years later she was rediscovered, largely due to the enthusiasm of Francis Wyndham. It was during those reclusive years that she had accumulated the stories collected in *Tigers are Better-Looking*. In 1966 she made a sensational reappearance with *Wide Sargasso Sea*, which won the Royal Society of Literature Award and the W. H. Smith Award in 1966 – her only comment on the latter being, 'It has come too late.' Her final collection of stories, *Sleep It Off Lady*, appeared in 1976 and *Smile Please*, her unfinished autobiography, was published posthumously in 1979. She was made a Fellow of the Royal Society of Literature in 1966 and a CBE in 1978. Jean Rhys died in 1979.

Jean Rhys

After Leaving Mr Mackenzie

Penguin Books

PENGUIN BOOKS

Published by the Penguin Group
Penguin Books Ltd, 27 Wrights Lane, London W8 5TZ, England
Penguin Books USA Inc., 375 Hudson Street, New York, New York 10014, USA
Penguin Books Australia Ltd, Ringwood, Victoria, Australia
Penguin Books Canada Ltd, 10 Alcorn Avenue, Toronto, Ontario, Canada M4V 3B2
Penguin Books (NZ) Ltd, 182–190 Wairau Road, Auckland 10, New Zealand

Penguin Books Ltd, Registered Offices: Harmondsworth, Middlesex, England

First published by Jonathan Cape 1930
Published by André Deutsch 1969
Published in Penguin Books 1971
10

Copyright 1930 by the Estate of Jean Rhys
All rights reserved

Printed in England by Clays Ltd, St Ives plc
Set in Monotype Baskerville

Contents

Part One

1. The Hotel on the Quay

After she had parted from Mr Mackenzie, Julia Martin went to live in a cheap hotel on the Quai des Grands Augustins. It looked a lowdown sort of place and the staircase smelt of the landlady's cats, but the rooms were cleaner than you would have expected. There were three cats – white Angoras – and they seemed usually to be sleeping in the hotel bureau.

The landlady was a thin, fair woman with red eyelids. She had a low, whispering voice and a hesitating manner, so that you thought: 'She can't possibly be a Frenchwoman.' Not that you lost yourself in conjectures as to what she was because you didn't care a damn anyway.

If you went in to inquire for a room she was not loquacious. She would tell you the prices and hand you a card:

HOTEL ST RAPHAEL
QUAI DES GRANDS AUGUSTINS
PARIS, 6me
CHAUFFAGE CENTRAL. EAU COURANTE
CHAMBRES AU MOIS ET À LA JOURNÉE

Julia paid sixteen francs a night. Her room on the second floor was large and high-ceilinged, but it had a sombre and one-eyed aspect because the solitary window was very much to one side.

The room had individuality. Its gloom was touched with a fantasy accentuated by the pattern of the wallpaper. A large bird, sitting on the branch of a tree, faced, with open beak, a strange, wingless creature, half-bird, half-lizard, which also had its beak open and its neck stretched in a belligerent attitude. The branch on which they were perched sprouted fungus and queerly shaped leaves and fruit.

The effect of all this was, oddly enough, not sinister but cheerful and rather stimulating. Besides, Julia was tired of striped papers. She had discovered that they made her head ache worse when she awoke after she had been drinking.

The bed was large and comfortable, covered with an imitation satin quilt of faded pink. There was a wardrobe without a looking-glass, a red plush sofa and – opposite the bed and reflecting it – a very spotted mirror in a gilt frame.

The ledge under the mirror was strewn with Julia's toilet things – an untidy assortment of boxes of rouge, powder, and make-up for the eyes. At the farther end of it stood an unframed oil-painting of a half empty bottle of red wine, a knife, and a piece of Gruyère cheese, signed 'J. Grykho, 1923'. It had probably been left in payment of a debt.

Every object in the picture was slightly distorted and full of obscure meaning. Lying in bed, where she was unable to avoid looking at it, Julia would sometimes think: 'I wonder if that picture's any good. It might be; it might be very good for all I know. . . . I bet it is very good too.'

But really she hated the picture. It shared, with the colour of the plush sofa, a certain depressing quality. The picture and the sofa were linked in her mind. The picture was the more alarming in its perversion and the sofa the more dismal. The picture stood for the idea, the spirit, and the sofa stood for the act.

2

Julia had come across this hotel six months before – on the fifth of October. She had told the landlady she would want the room for a week or perhaps a fortnight. And she had told herself that it was a good sort of place to hide in. She had also told herself that she would stay there until the sore and cringing feeling, which was the legacy of Mr Mackenzie, had departed.

At first the landlady had been suspicious and inclined to be hostile because she disapproved of Julia's habit of coming home at night accompanied by a bottle. A man, yes; a bottle, no. That was the landlady's point of view.

But Julia was quiet and very inoffensive. And she was not a bad-looking woman, either.

The landlady thought to herself that it was extraordinary a life like that, not to be believed. 'Always alone in her bedroom. But it's the life of a dog.' Then she had decided that Julia was mad, slightly pricked. Then, having become accustomed to her lodger, she had ceased to speculate and had gradually forgotten all about her.

Julia was not altogether unhappy. Locked in her room – especially when she was locked in her room – she felt safe. She read most of the time.

But on some days her monotonous life was made confused and frightening by her thoughts. Then she could not stay still. She was obliged to walk up and down the room consumed with hatred of the world and everybody in it – and especially of Mr Mackenzie. Often she would talk to herself as she walked up and down.

Then she would feel horribly fatigued and would lie on the bed for a long time without moving. The rumble of the life outside was like the sound of the sea which was rising gradually around her.

She found pleasure in memories, as an old woman might have done. Her mind was a confusion of memory and imagination. It was always places that she thought of, not people. She would lie thinking of the dark shadows of houses in a street white with sunshine; or of trees with slender black branches and young green leaves, like the trees of a London square in spring; or of a dark-purple sea, the sea of a chromo or of some tropical country that she had never seen.

Nowadays something had happened to her; she was tired. She hardly ever thought of men, or of love.

3

On Tuesday mornings at half-past nine, Liliane, the chambermaid, would bring up the letter from Mr Mackenzie's solicitor on the tray with coffee and a croissant.

She was a big, fair girl, sullen and rather malicious because she worked without stopping from six in the morning until eleven or twelve at night, and because she knew that, being plain, she would probably have to work like that until she died. Her eyes were small and hard in her broad face, and there were little pin-points of inquisitiveness in them like the pin-points of light in the pupils of a cat's eyes.

She would wish Julia good morning and then go out, banging the door, and on the tray would be the letter, typewritten in English:

Madame,

    Enclosed please find our cheque for three hundred francs (fcs. 300), receipt of which kindly acknowledge and oblige

Yours faithfully,
Henri Legros,
per N. E.

4

When Liliane had gone Julia opened her eyes unwillingly, bracing herself up. And this morning the letter was not there. Sometimes it did not come until a later post.

She drank her coffee. The curtains were still drawn. She turned on the electric light and began to read.

As she read a strained, anxious expression never left her face, which was round and pale with deep, bluish circles under the eyes. Her eyebrows were thin, finely marked; her very thick dark hair was lit by too red lights and stood out rather wildly round her head. Her hands were slender, narrow-palmed with very long fingers, like the hands of an oriental.

Her career of ups and downs had rubbed most of the hall-marks off her, so that it was not easy to guess at her age, her nationality, or the social background to which she properly belonged.

At twelve o'clock the maid knocked at the door and asked in a sullen voice when she could do the room.

'All right, all right,' Julia called. 'In half an hour.'

The central heating was not working properly and she felt cold. She dressed herself and then went and stood by the window to make up her face and to put kohl on her eyes, which were beautiful – long and dark, very candid, almost childish in expression.

Her eyes gave her away. By her eyes and the deep circles under them you saw that she was a dreamer, that she was vulnerable – too vulnerable ever to make a success of a career of chance.

She made herself up elaborately and carefully; yet it was clear that what she was doing had long ceased to be a labour of love and had become partly a mechanical process, partly a substitute for the mask she would have liked to wear.

To stop making up would have been a confession of age and weariness. It would have meant that Mr Mackenzie had finished her. It would have been the first step on the road that ended in looking like that woman on the floor above – a woman always dressed in black, who had a white face and black nails and dyed hair which she no longer dyed, and which had grown out for two inches into a hideous pepper-and-salt grey.

The woman had a humble, cringing manner. Of course, she had discovered that, having neither money nor virtue, she had better be humble if she knew what was good for her. But her eyes were malevolent – the horribly malevolent eyes of an old, forsaken woman. She was a shadow, kept alive by a flame of hatred for somebody who had long ago forgotten all about her.

Julia looked out of the window at the bookstalls on the quay. And beyond the bookstalls was the Seine, brown-green and sullen. When a river-boat passed, it would foam and churn up for a while. Then, almost at once, it was again calm and sluggish.

When she looked at the river she shivered. She felt certain that the water made her room much colder. It was only at night that she loved it. Then it seemed mysteriously to increase in width and the current to flow more strongly. When you were drunk you could imagine that it was the sea.

5

At one o'clock the maid knocked again.

'Yes, yes, yes,' said Julia fretfully.

Her coat was very old. She had grown fatter in the last few months and it was now too tight and too short for her. She imagined that it gave her a ridiculous appearance, especially behind. Indeed, her rare impulses towards activity vanished when she thought of her coat.

'I'm going out now,' she called.

It was drizzling. Julia walked quickly past the bookstalls and turned the corner by the big café on the Place St Michel. She stopped at the kiosk opposite and bought a newspaper.

She always lunched at a German restaurant in the Rue Huchette. When she came in the proprietor of the place wished her good morning from his strategic position on the stairs leading down to the kitchen. From there he could survey the waiters, the serving-up, and the legs of the women customers.

Julia took a seat at her usual table, propped her newspaper up in front of her and read it while she ate.

2. Mr Mackenzie

When she had finished her meal Julia went for a walk. She did this every day whatever the weather. She was so anxious not to meet anybody she knew that she always kept to the back streets as much as possible.

When she passed the café terraces her face would assume a hard forbidding expression, but she loitered by the shop-windows. Books and books, and again books. And then there would be windows exhibiting casts of deformed feet, stuffed dogs and foxes, or photographs of the moon.

That afternoon she stood for a long time in the Rue de Seine looking at a picture representing a male figure encircled by what appeared to be a huge mauve corkscrew. At the end of the picture was written, '*La vie est un spiral, flottant dans l'espace, que les hommes grimpent et redescendent très, très, très sérieusement.*'

She walked on towards the quay, feeling serene and peaceful. Her limbs moved smoothly; the damp, soft air was pleasant against her face. She felt complete in herself, detached, independent of the rest of humanity.

It was half-past four when she got back to her hotel and found Maître Legros' letter in the rack.

When she got up to her room she put the letter on the table. She was reluctant to open it. She wanted to retain her sense of well-being.

She lay down on the bed, lit a cigarette and watched the lights coming out in the Palais de Justice across the river like cold, accusing, jaundiced eyes.

The gramophone in the next room started. The young man who lodged there sometimes had a girl to see him, and then they would play the same record over and over again. Once, when Julia had passed the room, the door had been open. She had seen them together, the girl sitting by the young man's side and stroking his thigh upwards from the knee with a smooth, regular gesture; while he stared over her shoulder into vacancy, with an expression at once sensual and bored.

Julia got up and switched on the light. She read her letter:

Madame,

Enclosed please find our cheque for one thousand five hundred francs (fcs. 1,500). Our client has instructed us to make this final payment and to inform you that, from this date, the weekly allowance will be discontinued.

Kindly acknowledge receipt and oblige

Yours faithfully,
Henri Legros.

2

Julia unfolded the cheque. The words *'Quinze cents francs'* were written in a round, clear hand.

She had always expected that one day they would do something like this. Yet, now that it had happened, she felt bewildered, as a prisoner might feel who has resigned herself to solitary confinement for an indefinite period in a not uncomfortable cell and who is told one morning, 'Now, then, you're going to be let off today. Here's a little money for you. Clear out.'

Then she started to walk up and down the room with the palms of her hands pressed tightly together. She was planning her future in an excited and confused manner, for at that moment all sense of the exact value of the money had left her.

As she put on her hat she stared at herself in the looking-glass. She told herself, 'I must get some new clothes. That's the first thing to do.' And she longed for someone to whom she might say: 'I don't look so bad, do I? I've still got something to fight the world with, haven't I?'

The room already had a different aspect. It was strange

– as a place becomes strange and indifferent when you are leaving it.

Now the gramophone next door began to play again. . . . People were laughing, talking, pushing. Crowds of people were elbowing each other along a street, going to a fair. They pushed and laughed. And you heard the tramp of feet and the noise of the fair coming nearer; and the people calling. Then at last the noise of the crowd died away and you only heard the fair-music, vulgar, and yet lovely and strange.

When Julia got out into the street a certain caution awoke in her. She thought: 'I must go and sit somewhere and really make up my mind what I'd better do.'

She went into the café on the corner of the street; it was nearly empty. She sat down and ordered a drink. While she waited for it she looked at herself in the mirror opposite, still thinking of the new clothes she would buy.

She thought of new clothes with passion, with voluptuousness. She imagined the feeling of a new dress on her body and the scent of it, and her hands emerging from long black sleeves.

The waiter brought the Pernod she had ordered and she drank half the glass without adding any water. Warmth ran to her face and her heart began to beat more quickly.

She finished the drink. It seemed to her that it had left a bitter taste in her mouth. A heat, which was like the heat of rage, filled her whole body.

There was a blotter and pen-and-ink on the table before her. She opened the blotter and began to draw little flags on the paper. As she drew she was watching the face of Mr Mackenzie, which floated, wearing a cool and derisory smile, between her eyes and the blotter.

Suddenly a sensation of such dreary and abject humiliation overcame her that she would have liked to put her arms on the table and her head on her arms and to sob aloud, regardless of the people who might be looking at her or of what anybody might think.

She began to write a letter:

I got that cheque this afternoon. Why didn't you give me enough to go away when first I asked you? I am so horribly down now that I am absolutely good for nothing. And what do you think I can do with fifteen hundred francs, anyway?

At this point she stopped, realizing that she did not even know whether or not Mr Mackenzie were still in Paris. The last time she had seen him he was on the point of going away – for an indefinite time, he had said. . . . Besides, she was old enough to know that that sort of letter was never a bit of use, anyhow.

It was seven o'clock and the café was beginning to fill up. Julia went into the street and turned in the direction of the Boulevard Montparnasse.

3

The Boulevard St Michel was very crowded. Walking along blindly, Julia would bump every now and again into somebody coming in the opposite direction. When the people glared at her and muttered it seemed as if shadows were gesticulating.

The lights of the cafés were hard and cold, like ice.

When she had been walking for about twenty minutes she turned into a side-street, a narrow, rather deserted street of tall, quiet houses. Opposite number 72 she hesitated; then, instead of ringing the bell for the concierge, she crossed to the other side of the street and looked up at a window which she knew to be the window of Mr Mackenzie's bedroom. There was a light there. When she saw it she pressed her lips together with rather a grim expression.

She walked a few paces up and down the street, went back to a doorway opposite Mr Mackenzie's flat and stood there. Something in her brain that still remained calm told her that she was doing a very foolish thing indeed, and that the whole affair was certain to end badly for her. Nevertheless, she felt that she must see Mr Mackenzie. Six months of resignation were blotted out. She knew that she intended to wait until the occupant of the flat, who-ever it was, left it.

She had been standing there for perhaps half an hour when the light went out. Then, after an interval, the gate opposite opened and Mr Mackenzie came out into the street. He turned towards the Boulevard Montparnasse.

At the sight of him Julia's heart began to beat furiously and her legs trembled. She was excited to an almost un-bearable degree, for, added to her other emotions, was the fact that she was very much afraid both of him and of his lawyer. When she thought of the combination of Mr Mac-kenzie and Maître Legros, all sense of reality deserted her and it seemed to her that there were no limits at all to their joint powers of defeating and hurting her. Together the two perfectly represented organized society, in which she had no place and against which she had not a dog's chance.

She thought stubbornly, 'I don't care. I'm going to have it out with him. I don't care.'

When Mr Mackenzie was about twenty yards off she crossed over and followed him.

He made his way into the Boulevard Montparnasse and Julia saw him go into the Restaurant Albert.

4

Mr Mackenzie was a man of medium height and colour-ing. He was of the type which proprietors of restaurants and waiters respect. He had enough nose to look import-ant, enough stomach to look benevolent. His tips were not always in proportion with the benevolence of his stomach, but this mattered less than one might think.

Monsieur Albert asked if Monsieur were alone; and Mr Mackenzie answered, with a smile that he had trained not to be bashful, that he was quite alone that evening. Then

17

he ordered veau Clamart, which Monsieur Albert said was very good, and a carafe of red wine

Mr Mackenzie was comfortably off, but no millionaire. Helped by his father, who had owned a line of coastal steamers, and by a certain good luck which had always attended him, he had made his pile fairly early in life. He was not one of those people who regard the making of money as an adventure and cannot stop and do something else. He had made a fair sufficiency and then retired. He was forty-eight years old.

Paris had attracted him as a magnet does a needle. When in England he would always say, 'I like Paris, but I loathe the French.' When in Paris he disliked to be recognized as English, but at the same time, when he heard Frenchmen being funny about England, he would become hot and aggressive and would feel a righteous sense of betrayal.

He hid behind a rather deliberately absentminded expression. Once, in his youth, he had published a small book of poems. But when it came to actualities his mind was a tight and very tidy mind. He had discovered that people who allow themselves to be blown about by the winds of emotion and impulse are always unhappy people, and in self-defence he had adopted a certain mental attitude, a certain code of morals and manners, from which he seldom departed. He did depart from it, but only when he was practically certain that nobody would know that he had done so.

His code was perfectly adapted to the social system and in any argument he could have defended it against any attack whatsoever. However, he never argued about it, because that was part of the code. You didn't argue about these things. Simply, under certain circumstances you did this, and under other circumstances you did that.

Mr Mackenzie's code, philosophy or habit of mind would have been a complete protection to him had it not been for some kink in his nature – that volume of youthful poems perhaps still influencing him – which morbidly attracted him to strangeness, to recklessness, even un-happiness. He had more than once allowed himself to be drawn into affairs which he had regretted bitterly after-wards, though when it came to getting out of these affairs his business instinct came to his help, and he got out un-damaged.

5

Mr Mackenzie began to think about Julia Martin. He did this as seldom as possible, but the last time he had seen her had been in that restaurant. Now he remembered her un-willingly. That affair had ended very unpleasantly.

An insanity! Looking back on it, he thought, 'My God, why did I do it? Why did I want to sleep with her?' Yet there was no getting away from it; for a time she had obsessed him. He had lied; he had made her promises which he never intended to keep; and so on, and so on. All part of the insanity, for which he was not responsible.

Not that many lies had been necessary. After seeing him two or three times she had spent the night with him at a tawdry hotel. Perhaps that was the reason why, when he came to think of it, he had never really liked her.

'I hate hypocrites.' She had said that once. Quite casually.

He agreed. 'So do I,' he had said.

But he disliked the word 'hypocrite'. It was a word which he himself never used – which he avoided as if it had been an indecency. Too many senseless things were said by idiotic people about hypocrisy and hypocrites.

Yet she wasn't the hard-bitten sort. She was the soft sort. Anyone could tell that. Afraid of life. Had to screw herself up to it all the time. He had liked that at first. Then it had become a bit of a bore.

Julia had told him that she had married and had left England immediately after the armistice. She had had a child. The child had died – in Central Europe, somewhere – and then she had separated from her husband and had divorced him or been divorced by him, Mr Mackenzie could not gather which. Or perhaps she had never really been married at all. In any case she had come to Paris alone.

She had been an artist's model. At one time she had been a mannequin. But it was obvious that she had been principally living on the money given to her by various men. Going from man to man had become a habit. One day she had said to him, 'It's a very easy habit to acquire.'

On another occasion she had said, 'You see, a time comes in your life when, if you have any money, you can go one way. But if you have nothing at all – absolutely nothing at all – and nowhere to get anything, then you go another.'

He had thought that there was something in what she said, and yet he had not quite agreed with her. There would have been no end to the consequences of whole-hearted agreement.

He soon stopped asking intimate questions, because he knew that it was a mistake to be too curious about people who drift into your life and must soon inevitably drift out again. That wasn't the way to live.

The secret of life was never to go too far or too deep. And so you left these people alone. They would be pretty certain to tell you lies, anyhow. And they had their own ways of getting along, don't you worry.

He merely asked himself, as a man of the world, 'Does she, or does she not, get away with it?' And the answer was in the negative. She was at once too obvious and too obscure. The really incredible thing was that she did not seem to want to get away with it, that she did not seem to understand the urge and the push to get away with it at all costs. He knew, for instance, that she had not a penny of her own. After all that time she had not saved a penny.

Almost he was forced to believe that she was a female without the instinct of self-preservation. And it was against Mr Mackenzie's code to believe that any female existed without a sense of self-preservation.

She was irresponsible. She had fits of melancholy when she would lose the self-control necessary to keep up appearances. He foresaw that the final stage of her descent in the social scale was inevitable, and not far off. She began to depress him.

Certainly, she could be very sweet sometimes. But that's part of these people's stock-in-trade. You don't take any account of that.

He had always intended their parting to be a final one – these things had to come to an end. When he told her that he was going away, and that he proposed to present her with a certain sum of money weekly to give her time to rest, to give her time to look about her, etc., etc., she had answered that she did not want either to rest or to look about her. She had asked him to help her to get right away. But something which rose from the bottom of Mr Mackenzie's soul objected to giving her a lump sum of money, which of course she would immediately spend. Then, however much she might now protest to the contrary, she would come back for more.

He had abruptly refused, adding some scathing but truthful remarks.

Julia had wept; she had become hysterical. She had made a scene, sitting in that very restaurant, under the shocked and disapproving eyes of Monsieur Albert. She had made him look a fool.

A feeling of caution and suspicion which almost amounted to hatred had entirely overcome him. He had definitely suspected her of hoarding some rather foolish letters which he had written and which she had insisted that she had torn up. One of the letters had begun, 'I would like to put my throat under your feet.' He wriggled when he thought of it. Insanity! Forget it; forget it.

Caution was native to him – and that same afternoon he had placed the whole affair in the capable hands of Maître Legros – and he had not seen Julia since.

She haunted him, as an ungenerous action does haunt one, though Mr Mackenzie persisted in telling himself that he had not been ungenerous. Ungenerous! That was all nonsense.

Then he lifted his eyes from the veal – and there she was, coming in at the door.

6

She walked in – pale as a ghost. She went straight up to Mr Mackenzie's table, and sat down opposite to him. He opened his mouth to speak, but no words came. So he shut it again. He was thinking, 'O God, oh Lord, she's come here to make a scene. . . . Oh God, oh Lord, she's come here to make a scene.'

He looked to the right and the left of him with a helpless expression. He felt a sensation of great relief when he saw that Monsieur Albert was standing near his table and looking at him with significance.

'That's the first time I've ever seen that chap look straight at anybody,' Mr Mackenzie thought.

Monsieur Albert was a small, fair man, an Alsatian. His eyes telegraphed, 'I understand; I remember this woman. Do you want to have her put out?'

Mr Mackenzie's face instinctively assumed a haughty expression, as if to say, 'What the devil do you mean?' He raised his eyebrows a little, just to put the fellow in his place.

Monsieur Albert moved away. When he had gone a little distance, he turned. This time Mr Mackenzie tried to telegraph back, 'Not yet, anyhow. But stand by.'

Then he looked at Julia for the first time. She said, 'Well, you didn't expect to see me here, did you?'

She coughed and cleared her throat.

Mr Mackenzie's nervousness left him. When she had walked in silent and ghost-like, he had been really afraid of her. Now he only felt that he disliked her intensely. He said in rather a high-pitched voice, 'I'd forgotten that I had invited you, certainly. However, as you are here, won't you have something to eat?'

Julia shook her head.

There was a second place laid on the table. She took up the carafe of wine and poured out a glass. Mr Mackenzie watched her with a sardonic expression. He wondered why the first sight of her had frightened him so much. He was now sure that she could not make much of a scene. He knew her; the effort of walking into the restaurant and seating herself at his table would have left her in a state of collapse.

'But why do it?' thought Mr Mackenzie. 'Why in the name of common sense do a thing like that?'

Then he felt a sudden wish to justify himself, to let her know that he had not been lying when he had told her that he was going away.

He said, 'I only got back a couple of weeks ago.'

Julia said, 'Tell me, do you really like life? Do you think it's fair? Honestly now, do you?'

He did not answer this question. What a question, anyway! He took up his knife and fork and began to eat. He wanted to establish a sane and normal atmosphere.

As he put small pieces of veal and vegetable into his mouth, he was telling himself that he might just let her talk on, finish his meal, pay the bill, and walk out. Or he might accompany her out of the restaurant at once, under pretext of finding a quieter place to discuss things. Or he might hint that if she did not go he would ask Monsieur Albert to put her out. Though, of course, it was rather late to do that now.

At the same time he was thinking, 'No. Of course life isn't fair. It's damned unfair, really. Everybody knows that, but what does she expect me to do about it? I'm not God Almighty.'

She asked, 'How's your pal, Maître Legros?'

'Very well indeed, I think,' he said stiffly.

She began to talk volubly, in a low, rather monotonous voice. It was like a flood which has been long dammed up suddenly pouring forth.

He listened, half-smiling. Surely even she must see that

she was trying to make a tragedy out of a situation that was fundamentally comical. The discarded mistress – the faithful lawyer defending the honour of the client. . . . A situation consecrated as comical by ten thousand farces and a thousand comedies.

As far as he could make out she had a fixed idea that her affair with him and her encounter with Maître Legros had been the turning-point in her life. They had destroyed some necessary illusions about herself which had enabled her to live her curious existence with a certain amount of courage and audacity.

At the mention of Maître Legros Mr Mackenzie pricked up his ears, for he had only received three very businesslike communications from that gentleman, and he was rather curious to know how French lawyers manage these affairs.

She said that Maître Legros had bullied her about letters that she had destroyed and possible unpleasantness that she never intended to make.

Well, he probably had. For to put the fear of God into her was what he was paid for. On the other hand, if she had any sense she must have realized that three-quarters of it was a bluff.

She said that the lawyer had told his clerk to lock the door and send for an *agent*.

He wondered whether to believe this, for he had a vague idea that locking doors is one of the things that is not legal.

She said that he had threatened to have her deported, and had talked a great deal about the *police des mœurs*. She said that there had been a lot of clerks and typists in the room who had stared at her and laughed all the time.

'A lot?' he thought. 'Well, three or four at the outside.'

She said that she had begun to cry.

Well, in all careers one must be prepared to take the rough with the smooth.

She said that she had been determined never to accept the money offered.

'Well, well,' thought Mr Mackenzie. '*Tiens, tiens.*'

She said that she had fallen ill, and then she hadn't cared about anything except to lie in peace and be ill. And then she had written to the lawyer and asked for the allowance to be sent to her. And after that something had gone *kaput* in her, and she would never be any good any more – never, any more.

She raised her voice. 'Why did you pay a lawyer to bully me?' she said.

Mr Mackenzie pushed away his plate. This was intolerable. He could not go on pretending to eat – not if she were going to say that sort of thing at the top of her voice.

Besides, while she was talking, a chap whom he knew, a journalist called Moon, had come in with a friend, and was sitting two or three tables away. Moon was a gossip. He was talking volubly, and the friend, a thin, dark, youngish man, was glancing round the restaurant with rather a bored expression. At any moment the attention of these two might be attracted. Who knew to what wild lengths Julia would go?

Mr Mackenzie thought, 'Never again – never, never again – will I get mixed up with this sort of woman.'

His collar felt too tight for him. He thrust his chin out in an instinctive effort to relieve the constriction. The movement was exactly like that of a horse shying.

He looked at Julia and a helpless, imploring expression came into his eyes. His hand was lying on the table. She put her hand on his, and said, in a very low voice, 'You know, I've been pretty unhappy.'

At this change of attitude, Mr Mackenzie felt both relieved and annoyed. 'She's trying to get hold of me again,' he thought. 'But what a way to do it! My God, what a way to do it!'

He drew his hand away slowly, ostentatiously. Keeping his eyes fixed on hers, he deliberately assumed an expression of disgust. Then he cleared his throat and asked, 'Well, what exactly did you want when you came in here?'

Julia grew paler. The hollows under her eyes were deeper. She looked much older. But Mr Mackenzie had no pity for her; she was a dangerous person. A person who would walk in and make an uncalled-for scene like this was a dangerous person.

She said, 'Oh, yes, look here, this cheque . . . . This cheque I got today. I don't want it.'

'Good,' said Mr Mackenzie. 'Just as you like, of course. You're the best judge of that.'

But he felt surprised and not at all pleased. He knew that hysteria ruled these people's lives, but he would never have thought that it would be carried to the extremity of giving up money.

'Wait a minute,' she said. 'That isn't what I came here for.'

Mr Mackenzie was afraid of the expression in her eyes. He thought, 'My God, she's going to attack me. I ought to stop her.'

But, as it might have been in a nightmare, he could not do anything to stop her.

Assault! Premeditation could be proved. She wouldn't get away with it – not even here in Paris.

A cunning expression came into Julia's face. She picked up her glove and hit his cheek with it, but so lightly that he did not even blink.

'I despise you,' she said.

'Quite,' said Mr Mackenzie. He sat very straight, staring at her.

Her eyes did not drop, but a mournful and beaten expression came into them.

'Oh, well,' she said, 'all right. Have it your own way.'

Then, to Mr Mackenzie's unutterable relief, she gathered up her gloves and walked out of the restaurant.

7

Mr Mackenzie ate a few more mouthfuls of veal. By this time it was quite cold. But he wanted to gain time to compose himself.

Then he drank a little wine.

Then he looked round the room.

As he did so he was convinced that nobody had noticed anything. Not even Monsieur Albert, who had gone to the other side of the restaurant and was attending to a couple who had just come in.

Nobody had noticed anything.

Julia had not been in the restaurant for more than twelve minutes at the outside. His table was in a corner and she had sat with her back to the room. The last ghastly incident had happened so quickly that it was long odds against anybody having seen it.

Gradually Mr Mackenzie became calm. He felt he wanted some hot food.

He looked across the room, trying to attract Monsieur Albert's attention, and saw that the dark young man at the neighbouring table was staring at him with curiosity.

The dark young man instantly averted his eyes and his face assumed a completely blank expression – too blank.

'Hell!' thought Mr Mackenzie, 'that chap saw.'

But when Monsieur Albert had brought the hot food and another carate of wine he began to eat again, though without much appetite.

Then he began to pity Julia.

'Poor devil,' he thought. 'She's got damn all.'

3. Mr Horsfield

The name of the dark young man was George Horsfield. Half an hour afterwards he came out of the Restaurant Albert, thinking that he had spent a disproportionately large part of the last six months in getting away from people who bored him. (The last six months had been his kick of the heels.) The habit of wanting to be alone had grown upon him rather alarmingly.

He wondered whether it had been worth while to spend the only legacy he ever had, or was ever likely to have, in travelling about Spain and the south of France, because he had a vague idea that the sight of the sun would cure all his ills and would develop the love of life and humanity in which he felt that he was lamentably deficient.

Then he told himself that after all it had done him good; it had been worth while. He felt particularly well that evening; he felt in the mood to enjoy himself. He walked along slowly.

There was a tourist-car between the Dôme and the Rotonde. The small, black, pathetic figure of the guide stood mouthing and gesticulating.

Two women passed flaunting themselves; they flaunted their legs and breasts as if they were glad to be alive. There was zest in the air and a sweet sadness like a hovering ghost.

'Not sad,' Mr Horsfield thought. And then, 'Yes, but lots of these things are sad.'

He crossed the street and went into the Select-Bar for ten minutes. While he was sitting there, he remembered the quarrel he had seen in the Restaurant Albert and smiled to himself. The idea came to him, 'That woman's probably in one of these cafés having a drink.' He looked round; somehow he was pretty sure he would know her again.

There had been something fantastic, almost dream-like, about seeing a thing like that reflected in a looking-glass. A bad looking-glass, too. So that the actors had been slightly distorted, as in an unstill pool of water.

He had been sitting in such a way that, every time he looked up, he was bound to see the reflection of the back of Mr Mackenzie's head, round and pugnacious – somehow in decided contrast with his deliberately picturesque appearance from the front – and the face of the young woman, who looked rather under the weather. He had not stared at them, but he had seen the young woman slapping the man's face. He had gathered from her expression that it was not a caress, or a joke, or anything of that sort.

He had said, 'Good Lord.'

'What is it?' Moon had asked.

But the woman in the looking-glass seemed to be about to cry. Mr Horsfield felt uncomfortable. He averted his eyes, and replied, 'Oh, nothing, nothing.'

As she walked out of the restaurant he had turned to look after her, and asked, 'Do you know that woman?'

He said this because his companion claimed to know almost everybody in that quarter of Paris. He knew who lived with whom, and he could be illuminating on the subject of the Arts. He would say, 'D'you see that girl in the cocked hat and the top-boots? She's writing a novel about Napoleon.' Or, 'That man fiddling with his glass and muttering – he's really rather a genius. He's a sculptor; he reduces everybody's ego to an egg.'

However, Moon had been decidedly sniffy about the young woman. When he said, 'Oh, yes. I think I've seen her about at one time and another,' his tone put the strange creature so much in her place that Mr Horsfield felt rather ashamed of having expressed any kind of interest in her.

'A stolid sort of chap, Moon,' he thought, as he walked back down the boulevard, 'though jumpy on the surface. A bit of a bore, too.'

2

A little farther on Mr Horsfield went into another large and glaring café where a great many people were talking at the tops of their voices, mostly in German. He had a drink at the bar and then walked among the tables, found a vacant place, and sat down.

He looked about him, and saw the woman he had been thinking of sitting in a corner.

He recognized her hat – a dark-blue turban with a little veil hanging from the brim, but not low enough altogether to hide her eyes. He watched her, warming his glass of brandy in his hands. He felt detached and ironical.

She was sitting wedged against a very fat man with a

bald head. A lengthy tube, with a cigarette stuck in the end of it, protruded from the fat man's mouth. His expression was eager. He was obviously waiting for a friend. Every now and then he would get up and crane his neck in an attempt to keep his eye on all three entrances to the café.

Mr Horsfield thought that the young woman looked pretty lonely. He decided that, as soon as he could, he would go and sit at her table and try to talk to her.

The fat man got up and waved his hand violently at the door. Then he sat down again with a disappointed expression. Mr Horsfield finished his drink, and got the money to pay for it ready to leave on the table. He did not want any complications with the waiters.

An old chap at the next table was holding forth about Anglo-Saxons, and the phrase, '*cette hypocrisie froide*' came back and back into what he was saying. The word 'froide' sounded vicious and contemptuous. Mr Horsfield wanted to join in the argument, and say, 'Look here, you're quite wrong. Anyhow, you're not altogether right. What you take to be hypocrisy is sometimes a certain caution, sometimes genuine – though ponderous – childishness, sometimes a mixture of both.'

'*Ça vous écœure à la fin,*' jabbered the old chap. Rather a nice-looking old chap, too. All the more a pity.

The fat man at the young woman's table waved his arm again violently. He took the cigarette out of his mouth, smiled largely, and at last got up and hurried to meet his friend.

'D'you mind if I sit here?' Mr Horsfield asked.

'Of course, why not?' she said in an indifferent voice.

Mr Horsfield looked sideways at her. She was not so young as he had thought.

'I saw you in the restaurant where I was dining,' he said.

'You know Mackenzie, then?' she asked sharply.

'Not from Adam,' said Mr Horsfield. Then, because something in the place had momentarily freed him from self-consciousness, he added, 'I've been watching you. I thought you looked frightfully lonely.'

As he said this it occurred to him that as a rule he fought shy of lonely people; they reminded him too painfully of certain aspects of himself, their loneliness, of course, being a mere caricature of his own.

She said, 'Oh . . . Yes.'

Then she gulped at her drink and began to talk quite calmly and conversationally. Mr Horsfield rather admired the way she seemed to have been able to pull herself together.

She powdered her face. He thought that, for a moment, a furtive and calculating expression came into it.

She was telling him that she had not been to London for a very long time. 'I went back three years ago, but only for a fortnight.'

As she talked she looked at him unwinkingly, like a baby. Her eyes were very sad; they seemed to be asking a perpetual question. 'What?' thought Mr Horsfield. A deep black shadow painted on the outside of the corners accentuated their length.

She talked about a night-club in London which he knew had been going strong just before the war broke out. Mr Horsfield thought, 'She must be thirty-four or thirty-five if she's a day – probably older.' Of course, that explained a lot of things.

He interrupted something she was saying and, though he was not aware that he had done this with any accent of suspicion or scepticism, a sulky expression came over her face. She shrugged one shoulder a little and, without answering him, again relapsed into silence and indifference.

'But why should she be annoyed?' thought Mr Horsfield. 'Supposing I were to say to somebody, "I'm a hop factor; I own a small and decaying business," and he were to look incredulous. Should I be insulted? Not a bit of it. I shouldn't care a hoot.'

He wanted to laugh and say aloud, 'I'm a decaying hop

factor, damn you! My father did the growth and I'm doing the decay.'

After a time he suggested that they should go on to some dancing place.

'Oh, no,' she said. 'I can't. I don't want to.'

'Why not? Come on.'

'No,' she said obstinately, 'I'm not going to any of the Montparnasse places.'

Mr Horsfield said that they could go anywhere she liked. He would not care.

To his own ears his voice sounded slightly thickened. Yet he was not in the least drunk. He simply felt that he understood life better than he understood it as a general rule.

They went out and found a taxi. She gave the driver an address.

'Good,' said Mr Horsfield. 'Splendid.'

But he was not altogether happy. He missed in her the response to his own unusually reckless mood.

The taxi went a short distance up one street and down another, and then stopped. He thought, 'This place looks as if it has seen its best days.' Indeed it was unpretentious – even mediocre.

He was rather disappointed. However, he paid the driver and looked round for his companion.

'Well, good night,' she said. 'It isn't up to much here, but don't worry. You'll soon find a girl who'll show you something better.'

She was already walking along the street, which was dark, narrow, and inclined steeply up a little hill. He went after her and took her by the arm, feeling defrauded and extremely annoyed.

'But look here . . . '

'My clothes are too shabby.' She spoke in a passionate and incoherent way. 'I don't feel well. I don't feel up to it. My clothes are too shabby. . . . Besides, I hate people. I'm afraid of people. I never used to be like this, but now I'm going dippy, I suppose.'

'You were all right in the café just now,' he argued.

She pulled her arm away without answering. A young man passing by looked curiously at them and it flashed into Mr Horsfield's mind that they must seem like some sordidly disputing couple. If all this had happened in the daylight he would have been shamefaced and would have left her as soon as he decently could. But this deserted street, with its shabby, red-lit hotels, cheap refuges for lovers, was the right background for what she was saying.

'She's had a rum existence, this woman,' he thought, staring at her.

However, they could not stand there for ever. He felt very much at a loss.

He kept his arm in hers and they walked along together. They came to a cross-street, and he saw in the distance the Jewish twin-triangles illuminated as a sign over a cinema. He proposed with relief that they should go in.

'You won't mind sitting in a cinema, surely?'

'Oh, that cinema,' she said. 'It's rather a funny sort of place. I don't think you'd like it.'

'Never mind,' he said. 'Come along.'

3

An old woman peeped out of a little window and sold Mr Horsfield two tickets at three francs fifty each. Then they went into a large, bare hall where perhaps twenty people were scattered about, sitting on wooden seats.

They had come in during the interval, and a second old woman in a black dress was walking about the hall and occasionally upstairs into the balcony, calling out in a gentle voice: '*Cacahuètes . . . Pastilles de menthe. . . .* '

'It's always empty like this,' said Julia. 'I think those two old girls – the one outside and the one here – own it. I don't know, but I expect it will have to shut up soon.'

A loud clicking noise filled the emptiness. The lights went out and a strange, old-fashioned film flickered on the white screen. Someone began to play on a cracked piano.

'Valse Bleue', 'Myosotis', 'Püppchen'. . . . Mr Horsfield shut his eyes and listened to the pathetic voice of the old piano.

On the screen a strange, slim youth with a long, white face and mad eyes wooed a beautiful lady the width of whose hips gave an archaic but magnificent air to the whole proceeding.

After a while a woman behind them told the world at large that everybody in the film seemed to be *dingo*, and that she did not like films like that and so she was going out.

Mr Horsfield disliked her. He felt that in that bare place and to the accompaniment of that frail music the illusion of art was almost complete. He got a kick out of the place for some reason.

The film was German and rather good.

The noise of Julia blowing her nose jarred him like a light turned on suddenly in a room in which one is trying to sleep. Then, a sharp intake of her breath.

Of course, he might have known that that was what she would do.

But he felt that her sorrows were nothing whatever to do with him. On the contrary, he was the injured party. Ever since they had left the café she had been embarrassing and annoying him when all he wanted to do was to have a good time and not think. And God knew that he did not often feel like that.

He decided that when they left the cinema he would find out where she lived, get a taxi, take her home – and there would be the end of it. Once you started letting the instinct of pity degenerate from the general to the particular, life became completely impossible.

She caught her breath again. He put his hand out and felt for hers.

'Look here,' he said, 'please don't cry.'

She did not answer him.

'Will you come back to my hotel?' he asked. 'We can talk much better there.'

Then he got up and went out, knowing that she would follow.

Outside she walked along with her head bent. Her face was quite calm, and he wondered if indeed she had been crying or whether he had imagined it or whether she had meant him to imagine it.

They passed a little wine-shop where some men were having drinks at the bar. And then a dingy hotel. They reached the angle of the street where they had stood arguing.

A taxi passed. Mr Horsfield stopped it and told the man to drive to his hotel. The driver seemed rather sulky when he heard the address, probably because it was too near. However, Mr Horsfield settled the matter by getting firmly in, shutting the door and calling out in a loud voice, 'All right, go ahead.'

The driver started with a series of violent jerks. Then in an effort to relieve his bad temper, he shot off like an arrow from a bow.

She sighed deeply. Then she took from her bag a small gilt powder-box and began to powder her face carefully.

Mr Horsfield's mouth and throat were dry. He felt he wanted a long cool drink, and he remembered with relief the bottle of whisky and the syphon in his room.

4

There in his room was the tray with a syphon and glasses – two glasses, luckily. Mr Horsfield had locked the whisky away. He got it out and poured the drinks. Then he said: 'Perhaps you'd prefer some wine. Shall I get some wine up?'

She shook her head and began to sip mechanically.

'Well, here's luck,' said Mr Horsfield, sighing.

'Chin-chin,' said Julia. Over the rim of her glass her eyes looked cloudy and dazed.

'My God, it's hot in here,' he said. He opened the long

windows, which looked out on to the courtyard of the hotel. In one of the rooms opposite the light was on and he saw a young man and a girl embracing each other passionately.

He felt impatient. You couldn't get away from that sort of thing for a moment in this place.

He turned from the window and said: 'Tell me, are you stuck for money? Is that it?'

She opened her bag and took out two ten-franc notes and some small change.

'This is all I've got. I had a cheque for fifteen hundred francs but I went and gave it back.'

'I see. Quite,' said Mr Horsfield.

Then he thought that after all there was only one end to all this, and as well first as last. He opened his pocketbook. In it there were two notes for a thousand francs, one for five hundred, and some smaller money. He took out the five hundred and one of the thousand notes. They were creased carefully into four.

He put them into her hand and shut her fingers on them gently.

When he had done this he felt powerful and dominant. Happy. He smiled at Julia rather foolishly.

'Will that do you for a bit?' he asked. 'Will you be able to manage?'

'Yes,' she said. 'Thank you. You're very kind. You're kind and a dear.'

But he noticed that she took the money without protest and apparently without surprise, and this rather jarred upon him.

'Oh, that's all right,' he said.

The silence between them was an anti-climax.

Then it occurred to him that she might think that he had brought her to his room in order to make love to her. And he did not want to make love to her. That had all gone when she had started to cry and sniff in the cinema.

He felt embarrassed. You gave way to an impulse. You

36

did something you wanted to do – and then you were en-meshed in all sorts of complications.

He went and stood by the window again, tapping on the glass. His fingers were stained with cigarette smoking. Then he looked round and saw that Julia had taken off her hat. But she did not look in the glass and made no effort to arrange her hair.

She was certainly rather drunk. Her eyes were fixed as if upon some far-off point. She seemed to be contemplating a future at once monotonous and insecure with an in-difference which was after all a sort of hard-won courage.

For want of anything better to say, Mr Horsfield made a remark about Paris being a difficult place for Anglo-Saxons to be sober in.

She said: 'Oh, no place is a place to be sober in. That's what I think.'

This struck Mr Horsfield as being an extremely pathetic remark.

She began: 'After all . . . ' and then stopped. She had the look in her eyes of someone who is longing to explain herself, to say: 'This is how I am. This is how I feel.'

He suddenly remembered: 'Pa was a colonel. I was seduced by a clergyman at a garden-party. Pa shot him. Heavens, how the blighter bled!' He wanted to laugh.

He sat down by her side. 'Tell me,' he said gently.

'Well, I told you. I left London after the armistice. What year was that?'

'Nineteen-eighteen.'

'Yes. I left in February the year after. Then I wandered about a good deal with – with the man I left London with. Most places, but not Spain or Italy. And then I came along to Paris.'

'I see,' said Mr Horsfield encouragingly.

She said in a low voice, which was suddenly full of hatred: 'I was all right till I met that swine Mackenzie. But he sort of – I don't know – he sort of smashed me up. Before that I'd always been pretty sure that things would turn out all right for me, but afterwards I didn't believe in myself any more. I only wanted to go away and hide. Perhaps I was getting tired; perhaps I'd have smashed up anyway.'

Mr Horsfield thought: 'Well, nobody can go on for ever.'

But because he was rather drunk what she was saying seemed to him very intimate and close. He began to apply it to himself and he thought with anger. 'It's always like that. When you are tottering, somebody peculiarly well qualified to do it comes along and shoves you down. And stamps on you.'

'Well,' said Julia, 'that's that. And it's no use talking. And here's to a good life and a quick death. . . . When I'm drunk it's all right. Then I can think back and I know just why I did everything. It all falls into place, and I know that I couldn't have done anything else and that it's no use worrying.'

She sighed. 'But you can't be drunk the whole time.'

'You shouldn't sit and think too much,' Mr Horsfield said. 'You ought to get out and about and talk to people, not stay by yourself and brood.'

'Yes,' she said, 'of course.'

She stared at him, thinking: 'What's the use of trying to explain? It's all gone on too long.' Her mind went off at a tangent. She said: 'Well, it doesn't always help to talk to people. For instance. When I first came to Paris I used to sit to a woman, a sculptor – '

'You mean, when you first left England?'

'No, no,' she said in an impatient voice. 'I left England ages ago.'

Then her face assumed such a vague expression that Mr Horsfield thought: 'Well, go on, get on with it. If it's going to be the story of your life, get on with it.'

After a moment he prompted, 'Well, what about this woman you sat to?'

'I'd come from Ostend,' Julia explained. She spoke as if she were trying to recall a book she had read or a story she had heard and Mr Horsfield felt irritated by her vagueness, 'because,' he thought, 'your life is your life, and you must be pretty definite about it. Or if it's a story you are making up, you ought at least to have it pat.'

Then she brightened up, and added: 'I like Ostend. I like it very much. I was happy there, and I always remember places I was happy in. I mean, I remember them so that I can shut my eyes and be there. . . . We stayed at a little place called Coq-sur-Mer, near Ostend. And the water was cold and lovely. Yet not grey. And then I came along to Paris by myself. And then after a while I met this woman, and I started sitting for her. She gave me so much a week, and I used to go there nearly every day for as long as she wanted me.'

'Did you like her?' asked Mr Horsfield.

'I don't know if I liked her. I suppose so. She was all right in her way. Sometimes I liked her. Only she was all shut up. . . . And she thought that everything outside was stupid and that annoyed me. She was a bit fanatical, you know. She had something of an artist in her – I mean really. So, of course she was fanatical. And then she was a woman. About thirty-five years old. And so she simply wouldn't believe that anything was true which was outside herself or anything but what she herself thought and felt. She just thought I was stupid because it was outside her scheme of things that anybody like me should not be stupid. She thought me stupid and would say little things to hurt me. Like somebody flicking at you with a whip.

'Well, one day when we were having tea, because when it got too dark to work we would have tea and bread-and-butter and sometimes cake . . . I wish I could tell you how much I liked it, just having tea with her like that. . . .

'And so one day, when we were sitting smoking, and having tea, I started to tell her about myself. I was just going to tell her why I left England. . . . One or two things had happened, and I wanted to go away. Because I was fed up, fed up, fed up.

'I wanted to go away with just the same feeling a boy

has when he wants to run away to sea – at least, that I imagine a boy has. Only, in my adventure, men were mixed up, because of course they had to be. You understand, don't you? Do you understand that a girl might have that feeling?

'I wanted to get away. I wanted it like – like iron. Besides, I wasn't frightened of anything. So I did get away. I married to get away.

'Well, I told her all about that. And then, before I knew where I was, I was telling her everything else too. Everything that had happened to me, as far as I could.

'And all the time I talked I was looking at a rum picture she had on the wall – a reproduction of a picture by a man called Modigliani. Have you ever heard of him? This picture is of a woman lying on a couch, a woman with a lovely, lovely body. Oh, utterly lovely. Anyhow, I thought so. A sort of proud body, like an utterly lovely proud animal. And a face like a mask, a long, dark face, and very big eyes. The eyes were blank, like a mask, but when you had looked at it a bit it was as if you were looking at a real woman, a live woman. At least, that's how it was with me.

'Well, all the time I was talking I had the feeling I was explaining things not only to Ruth – that was her name – but I was explaining them to myself too, and to the woman in the picture. It was as if I were before a judge, and I were explaining that everything I had done had always been the only possible thing to do. And of course I forgot that it's always so with everybody, isn't it?'

Mr Horsfield said after a silence: 'Well, I think there's a good deal of tosh talked about free will myself.'

'I wanted her to understand. I felt that it was awfully important that some human being should know what I had done and why I had done it. I told everything. I went on and on.

'And when I had finished I looked at her. She said: "You seem to have had a hectic time." But I knew when she spoke that she didn't believe a word.'

40

There was another long pause. Then Mr Horsfield said: 'Didn't she? . . . Good Lord.'

Feeling this was inadequate, he added: 'She must have been rather an ass.'

'Yes,' said Julia. 'But it wasn't like that. Because I might have known she would be like that. It was a beastly feeling I got.'

She wrinkled up her forehead. She looked as if she were in pain.

'Well, don't worry about it now,' said Mr Horsfield. 'Have another whisky.'

'It was a beastly feeling I got – that I didn't quite believe myself, either. I thought: "After all, is this true? Did I ever do this?" I felt as if the woman in the picture were laughing at me and saying: "I am more real than you. But at the same time I *am* you. I'm all that matters of you."

'And I felt as if all my life and all myself were floating away from me like smoke and there was nothing to lay hold of – nothing.

'And it was a beastly feeling, a foul feeling, like looking over the edge of the world. It was more frightening than I can ever tell you. It made me feel sick in my stomach.

'I wanted to say to Ruth: "Yes, of course you're right. I never did all that. But who am I then? Will you tell me that? Who am I, and how did I get here?" Then I had just sense enough to pull myself together and not say anything so dotty.

'Then we went out to dinner. When I got home I pulled out all the photographs I had, and letters and things. And my marriage-book and my passport. And the papers about my baby who died and was buried in Hamburg.

'But it had all gone, as if it had never been. And I was there, like a ghost. And then I was frightened, and yet I knew that if I could get to the end of what I was feeling it would be the truth about myself and about the world and about everything that one puzzles and pains about all the time.'

She was swaying very slightly backwards and forwards, holding her knees, her eyes fixed.

Mr Horsfield was filled with a glow of warm humanity. He thought: 'Hang it all, one can't leave this unfortunate creature alone to go and drink herself dotty.'

He said: 'Now look here, I'm going to talk sense to you. Why don't you come back to London?'

She looked at him steadily with her large, unwinking eyes. She said: 'I don't know. I might go back to London. There's nothing to stop me.'

Then he thought: 'Good God, why in the world have I suggested that?' and added cautiously, 'I mean, you've surely got people there, haven't you?'

'Yes,' she said. 'Of course. My mother and my sister. But my mother's pretty sick. She's been ill for a long time.'

He felt that he could imagine what her mother and her sister were like. No money. No bloody money. Bloody money! You might well say 'Bloody money'. They would be members of the vast crowd that bears on its back the label, 'No money' from the cradle to the grave . . . And this one had rebelled. Not intelligently, but violently and instinctively. He saw the whole thing.

'I'm tired,' she said. And she was – very tired. Her excitement and the relief of having got some money were both swallowed up. She wanted to sleep. She felt very cold – the cold of drunkenness – as if something huge, made of ice, were breathing on her. She felt it most in her chest. But in spite of this her brain kept on working and planning in a worried fashion.

She said: 'You know, I've often thought of going back to London. Because I've got a friend there. I saw him again when I was in London three years ago. He'd help me. And goodness knows I want not to have to worry for a bit.' In a voice that was pathetically like a boast she added: 'He's a very rich man. He is . . . ' And then stopped.

'Good,' he said. 'Go ahead, then. Take a chance.'

'Nobody's ever said that I can't take a chance. That's the last thing anybody can say of me.'

He suddenly felt very sorry for her.

'If you do come to London,' he said, 'ring me up or write or something, will you? Here's my address.'

She took the card and said: 'Yes. All right.' And he thought, rather grimly: 'I bet you will . . .'

He saw her into a taxi.

It seemed to him that for a festive evening it had not been very festive.

The last thing in his mind before he went to sleep was:

> Roll me over on my right side,
>   Roll me over slow;
> Roll me over on my right side,
>   'Cause my left side hurts me so.

He did not know where or when he had heard this. For some reason it seemed to him peculiarly applicable to Julia.

4. The First Unknown

Liliane put the breakfast tray down on the end of the bed, and on going out, banged the door loudly.

Julia opened her eyes, remembering everything. She still felt fatigued and very anxious, and she opened her handbag to reassure herself by the sight of the money. She turned her head over on the pillow, shut her eyes, and saw herself slapping Mr Mackenzie's face. That seemed to have happened a long time ago. She knew that she would always remember it as if it were yesterday – and always it would seem to have happened a long time ago.

She thought: 'I must go away. That was a good idea. That's the only thing to be done.'

The difficulty was that she felt so tired. How to do all that must be done while she was feeling so tired?

She thought: 'If a taxi hoots before I count three, I'll go to London. If not, I won't.'

She counted, 'One . . . Two . . . ' slowly. A car shrieked a loud blast.

She drank her coffee and began to plan out how she would spend her fifteen hundred francs. So much was the least she must have on arrival in London, so much for her ticket, so much then was left for new clothes.

The idea of buying new clothes comforted her, and she got out of bed and dressed.

At three o'clock she was back at her hotel, carrying the boxes containing the clothes she had bought at a second-hand shop in the Rue Rocher – a dark grey coat and hat, and a very cheap dress, too short for the prevailing fashion.

She at once dressed herself in the new clothes, but the effect was not so pleasing as she had hoped. She fidgeted before the glass for a while, viewing herself from different angles. She began to reckon up the money she still had, and came to the conclusion that, on arriving in London, there would be about thirty shillings left.

Suddenly she began to doubt the wisdom of going there with so little money. She had no illusions as to the way in which her sister would receive her. It was pretty awful being in London without any money. Drabness swallowed you up, very quickly.

Then she told herself that she had made up her mind to go, and what was the use of all this chopping and changing?

My dear Norah,

I am in London. I don't know how long I'll stay, but I should like to see you. I have come over in a hurry or I would have let you know before. Will you telephone me or come to see me?

After she had finished her letter, which she intended to post in London, she began to pack her clothes. All the time she packed she was thinking: 'After all, I haven't

44

taken my ticket yet. I needn't go if I don't want to.'

A feeling of foreboding, of anxiety, as if her heart were being squeezed, never left her.

2

That night, coming back from her meal, a man followed her. When she had turned from the Place St Michel to the darkness of the quay he came up to her, muttering proposals in a low, slithery voice. She told him sharply to go away. But he caught hold of her arm, and squeezed it as hard as he could by way of answer.

She stopped. She wanted to hit him. She was possessed with one of the fits of rage which were becoming part of her character. She wanted to fly at him and strike him, but she thought that he would probably hit her back.

She faced him and said: 'Let me tell you, you are – you are . . .' The word came to her. 'You are *ignoble*.'

'Not at all,' answered the man in an aggrieved voice. 'I have some money and I am willing to give it to you. Why do you say that I am *ignoble*?'

They were now arrived at Julia's hotel. She went in, and pushed the swing-door as hard as she could into his face.

She could not have explained why, when she got to her room, her forebodings about the future were changed into a feeling of exultation.

She looked at herself in the glass and thought: 'After all, I'm not finished. It's all nonsense that I am. I'm not finished at all.'

3

Julia left Paris the next day by the midday boat train for Calais. She had bought an English illustrated paper at the Gare du Nord. In the train she read steadily down the glossy pages, which chattered about a world as remote and inaccessible as if it existed in another dimension.

The people sitting opposite to her – obviously a married

couple – were also English and they were reading the English papers. To all intents and purposes she was already in England. She felt strange and subdued.

In the wagon restaurant they were shown to the seats opposite to her, and they began to talk to the tall, fat man who was sitting next to Julia. He was a German. He seemed to be some sort of commercial traveller.

The couple had travelled from Marseilles on their return from somewhere in the Far East. They spoke in calm voices – cautiously. 'I think' or 'I believe' came into every sentence.

'Life out there has its disadvantages,' said the woman. 'But then, of course, it has its advantages, too.'

They were friendly people. They talked – or, rather, they answered the commercial traveller's questions – with volubility. But they always preserved a curious air of pale aloofness or perhaps of uncertainty.

The train swayed and the red wine jiggled about gaily in the glasses.

'Bombay?' said the man. 'Oh, yes, I remember Bombay. We managed to get a double-bedded room there.'

When the meal was over and they were all three back in the compartment the couple relapsed into silence. You could look for ever into their sunburnt faces and never be quite sure whether they were very kind or very hard, naïvely frank or very sly.

An hour from Calais the woman opposite took out a box of Mothersill's remedy for sea-sickness and swallowed differently coloured pills in accordance with the directions.

Julia planned that, on arriving at Victoria, she would get a taxi and ask the man to drive her to a cheap hotel in Bloomsbury. She hoped that she would get in somewhere quickly. The thought of driving from hotel to hotel alarmed her.

Then the throbbing of the train made her calm and sleepy, resigned as if she had taken some irrevocable step. She began to read her paper again. England. . . . English. . . . Our doggy page . . .

Part Two

1. Return to London

The taxi stopped at 33 Arkwright Gardens, WC. The street was dark and deserted as if it had been midnight instead of eight o'clock.

Julia said to the driver: 'Just wait a minute.' He did not answer or turn his head. He sat like a broad-shouldered image.

She went into the hotel.

'Will you show the lady number nine?' said the man at the bureau.

A young man, who had been sitting listlessly by the telephone, led the way upstairs and along a passage.

Number nine was small and very cold. There were an iron bedstead, an old-fashioned washstand with a tin slop-pail standing by the side of it, and a dressing-table with a wad of newspaper stuck into the frame to keep the glass at the required angle. The lace curtains were torn and very dirty. Behind the curtains was a green and optimistic sun-blind, faintly irritating, like a stupid joke.

The young man said: 'This room is eight-and-six a night, madam.'

'My God,' said Julia, 'what a place!'

The young man stared at her.

'All right. Very well.'

She opened her bag and took out a ten-shilling note with a slow and calculating gesture. She asked the young man to pay her taxi and bring up her luggage. He seemed surprised and looked at her, from the feet up. Then a knowing expression came into his face.

'Certainly, madam.'

In the passage he began to whistle shrilly: 'I Can't Give You Anything But Love, Baby.'

When he returned with her trunk Julia was standing at the looking-glass. He stared at her back inquisitively. She turned round and smiled at him.

'Your change, madam,' he said with austerity, averting his eyes.

She said she was very cold and she wanted to know how the gas-fire worked. The young man explained that it was a penny-in-the-slot meter, volunteered to let her have a shilling's worth, accepted an extra shilling for himself, smiled for the first time and departed.

She turned and looked into the glass again, sighed, and put her hand to her forehead with a worried gesture. Then she opened her trunk, found writing materials and began:

My dear Neil,

Would you write to this address and let me know when I can see you? Or would you telephone? I'll be very anxious until I hear from you. I hope you don't mind my writing to you. I hope you won't think of me as an importunate ghost.

She signed her name, wrote 'W. Neil James, Esq' on an envelope, hesitated a moment, and then added the address of a club.

A church clock chimed the hour. At once all feeling of strangeness left her. She felt that her life had moved in a circle. Predestined, she had returned to her starting-point, in this little Bloomsbury bedroom that was so exactly like the little Bloomsbury bedroom she had left nearly ten years before. And even the clock which struck each quarter in that aggressive and melancholy way was the same clock that she used to hear.

Perhaps the last ten years had been a dream; perhaps life, moving on for the rest of the world, had miraculously stood still for her.

The little old man in the bowler-hat who sold violets was at the corner of Woburn Square when she passed the next morning. While she was still some way off the idea that he might recognize her half pleased and half embarrassed her. She stopped and bought some flowers. He was just the same – shrunken, perhaps, under his many layers of dirty clothes. His light-blue eyes, which were like bits of glass, looked at her coldly. He turned his head away and went on calling: 'Violets, lady, violets,' in a thin, feeble voice.

She walked on through the fog into Tottenham Court Road. The houses and the people passing were withdrawn, nebulous. There was only a grey fog shot with yellow lights, and its cold breath on her face, and the ghost of herself coming out of the fog to meet her.

The ghost was thin and eager. It wore a long, very tight check skirt, a short dark-blue coat, and a bunch of violets bought from the old man in Woburn Square. It drifted up to her and passed her in the fog. And she had the feeling that, like the old man, it looked at her coldly, without recognizing her.

That cinema on the right-hand side. . . . She remembered going in there with a little Belgian when they had shown some town in Belgium being bombarded. And the little Belgian had wept.

During the war . . . My God, that was a funny time! The mad things one did – and everybody else was doing them, too. A funny time. A mad reckless time.

An exultant and youthful feeling took possession of her. She crossed Oxford Street into Charing Cross Road. But in Soho she missed her way and her exultation suddenly vanished. She began to think that she must look idiotic, walking about aimlessly. She found her way back into Oxford Street and went into Lyons'.

A band filled the vast room with military music, played at the top of its voice. Grandiose. . . .

At the table where she sat down two rather battered-looking women with the naïve eyes of children were eating steak-and-kidney pudding. One said to the other: 'This place is on a big scale, you can't deny that.'

Her companion agreed, and said that she thought the ladies' room very fine – all in black-and-white marble.

The two women left quickly. They melted away, as it were, and their place was taken by a little man who, in the midst of his meal, uttered an exclamation, seized his bill, and rushed off.

'Your gentleman friend has left his hat behind,' said the waitress amiably.

'Oh, has he?' said Julia. She began to put on her gloves.

When she looked up the little man was once more seated opposite her. He said excitedly: 'A most extraordinary thing! I've just seen a man I thought was dead. Well, that's an extraordinary thing. A thing like that doesn't happen every day to anybody, does it? A man I thought was killed in the Japanese earthquake.'

'Were you pleased to see him?' asked Julia.

'Pleased to see him?' echoed the little man cautiously. 'Well, I don't know. But it gave me a bit of a turn, I can tell you.'

Julia left him talking to the waitress, who was making clicking, assenting noises with her tongue.

It was three o'clock, and before each of the cinemas a tall commissionaire was calling: 'Plenty of seats. Seats at one-and-two. Plenty of seats.'

Vague-looking people hesitated for a moment, and then drifted in, to sit in the dark and see *Hot Stuff from Paris*. The girls were perky and pretty, but it was strange how many of the older women looked drab and hopeless, with timid, hunted expressions. They looked ashamed of themselves, as if they were begging the world in general not to notice that they were women or to hold it against them.

The porter told her when she got back to the hotel that Miss Griffiths was waiting for her upstairs.

'She's been there nearly half an hour,' he said.

2. Norah

Norah Griffiths was a tall, dark girl, strongly built and straight-backed.

'Hullo, Norah, my dear,' said Julia.

'Hullo, Julia.'

They both hesitated, then both at the same moment bent forward to kiss each other. Norah gave her sister one rapid, curious glance. Then she sat down again, looking calm and as though she were waiting for explanations. Her head and arms drooped as she sat. She was pale, her colourless lips pressed tightly together into an expression of endurance. She seemed tired.

Her eyes were like Julia's, long and soft. Fine wrinkles were already forming in the corners. She wore a pale-green dress with a red flower fixed in the lapel of the collar. But the dress had lost its freshness, so that the flower looked pathetic.

'Well, I got your letter this morning, and I thought I'd come along at once,' she said.

She had a sweet voice, a voice with a warm and tender quality. This was strange, because her face was cold, as though warmth and tenderness were dead in her.

Julia, who felt very nervous, fidgeted about the room. She took off her hat, powdered her face, rouged her lips. Norah followed her every movement with an expression of curiosity.

Julia sat down on the bed and began: 'I decided to come over very suddenly.'

Then she stopped. 'If a car hoots before I count three, I'll do this. If it doesn't, I'll do that . . . ' To know that this was the only reasonable way to live was one thing; to explain and justify it to somebody else – especially to Norah – was quite another.

Norah asked: 'Are you going to stay for long?'

'I don't know.'

Then there was a silence, like that between travellers in a railway carriage who have started a conversation which dies from lack of subjects of mutual interest.

Julia asked how their mother was, and Norah answered that she was much the same. 'The doctor says she's getting weaker, but I don't see any difference myself.'

'When may I come to see her?'

'She won't know you,' Norah said. 'You realize that, don't you? She doesn't know anybody. However, come whenever you like. Come tomorrow afternoon.'

'It doesn't bear thinking of,' Julia said miserably.

She had been accustomed for years to the idea that her mother was an invalid, paralysed, dead to all intents and purposes. Yet, when Norah said in that inexorable, matter-of-fact voice: 'She doesn't know anybody,' a cold weight descended on her heart, crushing it.

Norah agreed. 'The way people die doesn't bear thinking of.'

Julia said: 'That chair's awfully uncomfortable. Won't you sit on the bed near me, and let's talk?'

She made an awkward gesture. Her eagerness made her awkward. She had been longing for some show of affection, or at any rate of interest, but Norah kept looking at her as if she were something out of the zoo. She felt an answering indifference, and at the same time pain and a tightness of the throat.

She wanted to say: 'Do you remember the day I took off my shoes and stockings when we were paddling and carried you because the pebbles hurt your feet? Well, I've never forgotten that day.'

'I can't stay for very long,' said Norah without moving, 'because I'm going to see Uncle Griffiths. He's in London now, and he always asks me to tea when he comes.'

'Oh, does he?' said Julia. 'Kind man!'

Norah said calmly: 'Yes, I think he is kind.'

When she had read Julia's letter she had said: 'You'll never guess who's turned up again. . . . Well, I suppose I'd better go along and see her.' She was feeling curious, even pleased. Because something fresh was always something fresh – a little excitement to break the monotony.

But now all her curiosity had departed and she only wanted to get away. Her first sight of Julia had shocked her, for it seemed to her that in the last three years her sister had indisputably changed for the worse.

She thought: 'She doesn't even look like a lady now. What can she have been doing with herself?'

Norah herself was labelled for all to see. She was labelled 'Middle class, no money.' Hardly enough to keep herself in clean linen. And yet scrupulously, fiercely clean, but with all the daintiness and prettiness perforce cut out. Everything about her betrayed the woman who has been brought up to certain tastes, then left without the money to gratify them; trained to certain opinions which forbid her even the relief of rebellion against her lot; yet holding desperately to both her tastes and her opinions.

Her expression was not suppressed or timid, as with so many of her kind. Her face was dark and still, with something fierce underlying the stillness.

She said: 'D'you know, I'm afraid I must go now. What time will you come round tomorrow?'

'Look here, Norah,' said Julia, 'it isn't that I want to bother you, but I came over without much money. I've only got a little over a pound left. I won't be able to stay in this place much longer.'

Norah opened her eyes widely, and said in a cold voice: 'I've got eight pounds, and that's got to last for a month, and the doctor comes nearly every day. Count up for yourself.'

'I know,' said Julia eagerly, 'I know. I don't want you to lend me money. I know perfectly well that you can't. I simply thought you might let me stay at the flat for a few days, till I get an answer from a man I've written to.'

Norah's expression confused her, and she went on, raising her voice: 'I'll be quite all right in a week or so. Only he may be away. He may not be able to answer at once.'

'I'm awfully sorry,' Norah replied coldly, 'but I've got a friend staying with me – Miss Wyatt, she's a trained nurse. I can't turn her out at a moment's notice, can I? And there's not a scrap more room in the place.'

'Oh, I see,' said Julia. She sighed. She stretched her legs out and put her head on the pillow. 'Well, all right. There's a light outside. Mind you put it on as you go out, or you may fall down those stairs.'

'Yes, but look here, this is perfectly absurd,' said Norah fretfully. 'You've had practically nothing to do with us for years – and you don't seem to have starved.'

Julia did not answer.

'And who's better dressed – you or I?' said Norah. A fierce expression came into her eyes.

Julia said, bursting into a loud laugh: 'Yes, d'you know why that is? Just before I came over here I spent six hundred francs on clothes, because I thought that if I was too shabby you'd all be ashamed of me and would give me the cold shoulder. Of course, I didn't want to risk that happening, did I?'

'You're an extraordinary creature,' said Norah.

Something in her voice enraged Julia, who began to argue rather incoherently: 'Why should you be like this? What do you blame me for – exactly?'

'But I don't blame you,' said Norah. 'I don't consider that what you do is any business of mine. Besides, I'm far past blaming anybody for anything. Oh, yes, I've got far past that stage, believe me. . . . I simply said I thought it very very odd of you to turn up here at a moment's notice and to send for me and expect that I can produce money for you.'

'Oh, God!' said Julia loudly. 'But it wasn't money I wanted.'

She went on in a totally different voice: 'Well, it doesn't matter, anyway.'

Standing at the door, a feeling of compunction touched Norah. She looked round the room and said: 'This really is an awful place. Why on earth do you come to a place like this?'

'Yes, look at it,' said Julia, suddenly bitter. 'Look at those filthy curtains. My God, foreigners must have a fine idea of London – coming to hotels like this. No wonder they avoid it like the plague.'

Norah did not answer this, because the opinion which foreigners might have of London was a matter of complete indifference to her. She said: 'Why don't you go to a boarding-house?'

Then she added, for the sake of something to say: 'Uncle Griffiths' place is awfully comfortable. He's at a boarding-house at Bayswater. A private hotel place.'

'Oh, is he?' said Julia. 'What's his address?'

Norah told her. Then the thought came to her: 'I hope to God she won't go and ask him for money.' And she added suspiciously: 'Why do you want to know?'

'Oh, nothing,' said Julia. 'Well . . . I'll come along tomorrow.'

'All right. Good-bye,' said Norah.

'Good-bye.'

2

'Well, I suppose I've changed too,' thought Julia. 'I suppose I look much older, too.'

She began to imagine herself old, quite old, and forsaken. And was filled with melancholy and a terror which was like a douche of cold water, first numbing and then stimulating. She lit a cigarette and began to walk up and down the room.

She had lost the feeling of indifference to her fate, which in Paris had sustained her for so long. She knew herself ready to struggle and twist and turn, to be unscrupulous and cunning as are all weak creatures fighting for their lives against the strong.

Of course, say what you like, London was a cold and

terrifying place to return to like this after ten years. She told herself that after all the idea of going to a boarding-house was a good idea. There she would have bed and food for a week without any need to bother.

She made anxious calculations and decided that with about another couple of pounds she would be all right.

The thing was to keep calm and try everything possible. She found Mr Horsfield's card in her bag.

At the telephone she became very nervous. Mr Horsfield was not able to hear what she was saying, and this made her still more nervous. The man at the bureau was looking at her. Julia fixed him with a cold and defiant stare.

'Oh, yes,' said Mr Horsfield. 'Yes, yes. . . . Of course . . .'

Then there was a long pause while he was making up his mind. He was thinking: 'That woman! I suppose I did give her my address. Well, she hasn't been long about turning up.' He wished he could remember more clearly what she looked like. Then, as invariably happened, he gave way to his impulse.

'Hullo,' he said. 'Are you there?'

'Yes,' said Julia.

When he asked her if she would dine with him that night she answered: 'Yes,' smiling at the telephone.

'Where are you staying?' he said. 'I'll call for you about eight o'clock if I may.'

She told him her address and rang off. It was just after four o'clock.

3. Uncle Griffiths

Julia's Uncle Griffiths was dressing for dinner when the page-boy knocked and told him that there was a lady downstairs who wished to see him. The page's face was serious, but something about his intonation suggested a grin.

'A lady?' said Mr Griffiths, in a voice which sounded alarmed and annoyed, as he might have said: 'A zebra? A giraffe?'

He was about sixty-five years of age, looking a good ten years younger. His face was short, broad, almost un-wrinkled, red – but not unhealthily so. His hair was white. His eyes were pale-blue and cold as stones.

The page-boy said: 'I told the lady I wasn't quite sure if you were in, sir.'

Mr Griffiths turned to his wife and said in a resigned voice: 'That must be Julia.'

'Ask her if she'd mind waiting a few minutes,' he told the boy.

Julia waited in a large, lofty room, crowded with fat, chintz-covered arm-chairs. Two middle-aged women were sitting by the fire talking. They looked comfortable and somnolent. But Julia sat outside the sacred circle of warmth. She was cold, and held her coat together at the throat. The coat looked all right but it was much too thin. She had hesitated about buying it for that reason, but the woman in the second-hand shop had talked her over.

She thought: 'Of all the idiotic things I ever did, the most idiotic was selling my fur coat.' She began bitterly to remember the coat she had once possessed. The sort that lasts for ever, astrakhan, with a huge skunk collar. She had sold it at the time of her duel with Maître Legros.

She told herself that if only she had had the sense to keep a few things, this return need not have been quite so ignominious, quite so desolate. People thought twice be-fore they were rude to anybody wearing a good fur coat; it was protective colouring, as it were.

She began to regret having come. And yet why should she not have come? Uncle Griffiths had always seemed to like her. Once when she was a child he had said that she was pretty, and this had thrilled her. At that time he had represented to the family the large and powerful male. She did not remember her father well; he had died when she was six and Norah a baby of one.

Uncle Griffiths came in and she got up eagerly. He said: 'Well, Julia,' and put out a stiff and warming hand. 'Come along upstairs to my room, will you?'

On the staircase he said: 'No use talking in there, with people listening to every word you say.'

He gripped the upper part of her arm to guide her along the passage.

'Oh, yes, very well – very well indeed,' she replied to his questions, still smiling mechanically.

In the bedroom he introduced Julia to his wife, who said in a placid voice that she had better leave them to talk, hadn't she?

She was his second wife. He had met her at a small hotel at Burnham-on-Crouch and had married her without knowing anything about her. It was the one impulsive action of his life, and he had never regretted it.

'Sit down,' said Uncle Griffiths.

Julia sat down. Uncle Griffiths stood with his back to the fire, sucking at his white moustache and staring at her. He looked inquisitive but cautious – slightly amused, too, as if he were thinking: 'Now, then, what have you been up to? Of course, I know what you've been up to.'

To Julia he appeared solid and powerful, and she felt a great desire to please him, to make him look kindly at her.

Uncle Griffiths cleared his throat and said: 'I was very much surprised to hear from Norah that you were in London, Julia. I thought that you were quite settled in – where was it?'

Julia said that she had been in Paris.

'Dear me,' said Uncle Griffiths. 'Was it Paris?'

All the furniture in the room was dark, with a restful and inevitable darkness; and sombre curtains hung over the windows. The long, thin flames of the fire sprang from an almost solid mass of coal.

She said: 'I left on Thursday. It's funny, for it seems much longer ago than that.'

'I see,' said Uncle Griffiths. 'So you made up your mind to come over and pay us a flying visit, did you?'

But this was merely rhetoric. He had summed her up. He knew, both from what Norah had told him and from his own observation, that she had made a mess of things and was trying to get hold of some money.

She said: 'I don't know why I came. A sort of impulse I suppose.'

'Good God,' said Uncle Griffiths. His voice always sounded as if he were speaking between closed teeth. 'If I were you,' he went on, 'I should go back again. Things are very difficult over here, you know. Hard. Yes, yes – hard times.'

She said: 'I daresay, but you see, I haven't any money to go back with.'

Uncle Griffiths considered her for some seconds without speaking, and then said: 'Do you know where your husband is?'

Julia said in a low voice: 'You know. . . . I thought you knew. . . . I left him. I don't know where he is now. He went absolutely smash, you know.'

'He was a damned bad lot,' said Uncle Griffiths.

'He wasn't,' said Julia sullenly.

She felt as though her real self had taken cover, as though she had retired somewhere far off and was crouching warily, like an animal, watching her body in the arm-chair arguing with Uncle Griffiths about the man she had loved.

'What?' said Uncle Griffiths loudly. 'He married you and left you stranded, and then you tell me that he wasn't a bad lot?'

'He didn't leave me,' argued Julia. 'I left him.'

'Nonsense,' said Uncle Griffiths.

He thought: 'Why should I have to bother about this woman?' But some vague sense of responsibility made him go on asking questions.

He said: 'I thought he was supposed to have some money. He must have had some money, gallivanting about as you did. Why didn't you make him settle something on you?'

'When he had money, he gave me a lot,' said Julia. She added in a low voice: 'He gave me lovely things – but really lovely things.'

'I never heard such nonsense in my life,' said Uncle Griffiths sturdily.

Suddenly, because of the way he said that, Julia felt contemptuous of him. She thought: 'I know you. I bet you've never bought lovely things for anybody. I bet you've never given anybody a lovely thing in your life. You wouldn't know a lovely thing if you saw it.'

Because she felt such contempt her nervousness left her.

Her uncle said he wasn't going to argue with her, and that he couldn't imagine what good she thought she would do by coming over to England, and that he was astounded when he heard that she had come – astounded, because he had understood that she had some sort of job in Paris, or wherever it was, and jobs were not easy to get in London. He said that he had not got any money and that if he had he would not give it to Julia, certainly not, but to her sister Norah, and that he would like to help Norah, because she was a fine girl, and she deserved it.

'But the truth is that I haven't got any money to give to anybody,' he said. 'In fact, if things go on as they are going now, goodness knows what'll become of me.'

An anxious expression spread over his face as he thought to himself that the time was coming when he would have to give up this comfort, and then that comfort, until God knew what would be the end of it all. In his way he was an imaginative man, and when these fits of foreboding overcame him he genuinely forgot that only a succession of highly improbable catastrophes could reduce him to the penury he so feared.

Julia was thinking that she might try to pawn something and that she had forgotten where the pawnshops were. There was one in a side-street near Leicester Square – Rupert Street, wasn't it? Silver things in the window. But anyhow what had she to pawn that would fetch even a few shillings?

Uncle Griffiths was still talking: 'You always insisted on going your own way. Nobody interfered with you or expressed any opinion on what you did. You deserted your family. And now you can't expect to walk back and be received with open arms.'

'Yes,' she said, 'it was idiotic of me to come. It was childish, really. It's childish to imagine that anybody cares what happens to anybody else.'

He chuckled, and said with an air of letting her into a secret and an expression that was suddenly open and honest: 'Of course, everybody has to sit on their own bottoms. I've found that out all my life. You mustn't grumble if you find it out too.'

Then he said: 'I tell you what I'll do. I'll give you a pound to help you pay your fare back to Paris.'

He brought out a pocket-book, and handed her a note. She took it, put it into her bag, immediately got up, and said: 'Good night.'

Uncle Griffiths, looking more cheerful now that the interview was over, answered: 'Good night,' and put his hand out kindly. Julia walked past him without taking it, and he put it back into his pocket, and said: 'Take my advice. You get along back as quickly as you can.'

2

Julia felt bewildered when she got into the street. She turned and walked without any clear idea of the direction she was taking. Each house she passed was exactly like the last. Each house bulged forward a little. And before each a flight of four or five steps led up to a portico supported by two fat pillars.

Down at the far end of the street a voice quavered into a melancholy tune. The voice dragged and broke – failed. Then suddenly there would be a startlingly powerful bellow, like an animal in pain. The bellow was not fierce or threatening, as it might have been; it was complaining and mindless, like an animal in pain.

Julia thought: 'They might light the streets a bit better here.'

It was the darkness that got you. It was heavy darkness, greasy and compelling. It made walls round you, and shut you in so that you felt you could not breathe. You wanted to beat at the darkness and shriek to be let out. And after a while you got used to it. Of course. And then you stopped believing that there was anything else anywhere.

The singer – a drably vague figure standing as near as he dared to the entrance to a public bar – had started *The Pagan Love Song* for the second time.

The buses would stop near the pub.

She got on the next one that was going in the direction of Oxford Circus, mounted to the top, and sat there with her eyes shut.

4. Café Monico

Mr Horsfield was waiting for her. Julia went up to him and said: 'I'm afraid I'm late.'

'Not at all.'

He shook hands without smiling, then looked away from her instantly, his face assuming an expression of detached politeness.

As they waited in the street for a taxi he looked sideways at her, coldly. A sensation of loneliness overcame her. She thought that there was something in the expression of the eyes of a human being regarding a stranger that was somehow a dreadful give-away.

They got into the taxi.

'My God,' she muttered, 'what a life! What a life!'

'I expect London's depressing you,' said Mr Horsfield.

'It's a bit dark, when one comes back to it.'

There was a pause. Then he asked: 'Do you like sherry? I hope you do, because the sherry at this place we're going to is rather good.'

He looked very tidy and very precise. He looked the sort that never gives itself away and that despises people who do, that despises them and perhaps takes advantage of them. He would think: 'Poor devil.' Yes, he might go so far as to think like that, but the poor devil would remain a poor devil whom you theorized about but never tried to understand.

Julia thought: 'He's been taught never to give himself away. Perhaps he's had a bad time learning it, but he's learnt it now all right.'

He was hollow-cheeked. His mouth drooped at the corners – not bad-temperedly, but sadly. He looked rather subdued, till you saw in his eyes that he was not quite subdued yet, after all.

He said: 'Well, do you like the sherry?'

'No, not terribly.'

'Then we'll try something else.'

They sat at a table near the window, and were waited on by a tall, fat, pale Frenchman with a Bourbon nose who was pompous and superior to the verge of bursting. His fat white face and his little scornful eyes irritated Julia. She thought that she would like to turn round and say something rude to him. Just one word – one little word – to see the expression on his face when she said it.

Then food and the rosy lights comforted her. She began to feel aloof and she forgot the waiter.

Mr Horsfield talked politely. He was trying to find out what was expected of him, but she answered him vaguely and absent-mindedly in monosyllables.

She wanted to attract and charm him. She still realized that it might be extremely important that she should attract and charm him. But she was unable to resist the dream-like feeling that had fallen upon her which made what he was saying seem unreal and rather ludicrously unimportant.

When they were drinking coffee, she said, 'My hotel's a dreadful place. I hate it.'

'I don't wonder,' said Mr Horsfield. 'Why did you go there?'

Julia explained: 'The taxi-man took me. I said to him: "Take me to a quiet hotel, not expensive, in Bloomsbury." Because, you see, I was afraid of having to go from one place to another and I didn't remember where I could go. He sort of eyed me, and then he took me there.'

Mr Horsfield said: 'I'll find you a better place than that.' He asked: 'I suppose you've made up your mind to stay for some time?'

'I don't know,' said Julia. 'I've no idea. I don't really know at all.' And then she once more remembered that, when she had rung him up, she had intended to explain her situation and ask him to help her.

She realized with a shock that the meal was nearly over. She thought: 'If I'm going to do it at all I must do it now.'

She felt nervous and shivered.

'I'm awfully cold,' she said.

It was stupid that, when you had done this sort of thing a hundred times, you still felt nervous and shivered as you were doing it.

Mr Horsfield stared at her and said: 'What's the matter? Are things going badly?' He thought: 'After all, fifteen hundred francs isn't much. Fancy having to rely for good and all on fifteen hundred francs!' And then he thought: 'Oh, God, I hope she's not going to cry.'

He said: 'Look here, let's go somewhere else and talk. Don't tell me about things here. We'll go somewhere else to talk.'

She said, speaking quickly: 'You surprised me, because people nearly always force you to ask, don't they?'

'They do,' said Mr Horsfield.

Her face was red. She went on talking in an angry voice: 'They force you to ask – and then they refuse you. And then they tell you all about why they refuse you. I suppose they get a subtle pleasure out of it, or something.'

Mr Horsfield said: 'Subtle pleasure? Not at all. A very simple and primitive pleasure.'

'It's so easy to make a person who hasn't got anything seem wrong.'

'Yes,' he said. 'I know. That's dawned on me once or twice, extraordinary as it may seem. It's always so damned easy to despise hard-up people when in one way and another you're as safe as houses. . . . Have another liqueur.'

But he was relieved when she declined, because he was afraid she looked rather drunk. He watched her anxiously, feeling all at once very intimate with her. And he hated the feeling of intimacy. It made something in him shrink back and long to escape.

She made her inevitable, absent-minded gesture of powdering her face. She looked happier, and relieved. That, of course, was because she imagined that she was now going to cast all her woes on his shoulders. Which was all very well, he thought, but he had his own troubles.

3

When he took her arm to pilot her across Regent Street he touched her as lightly as possible. They turned to the right and walked along aimlessly.

Julia thought: 'This place tells you all the time, "Get money, get money. get money, or be for ever damned." Just as Paris tells you to forget, forget, let yourself go.'

Mr Horsfield said, in an aimless voice: 'Now, let me see, where shall we go?'

'This will do as well as anywhere, won't it?'

They were passing the Café Monico. She walked in, and he followed her. When they had sat down she said: 'I hate drifting about streets. Do you mind? It makes me awfully miserable.'

Then she said that she would have a *fine*. And Mr Horsfield ordered a *fine* and a whisky and watched her drinking.

She looked older and less pretty than she has done in Paris. Her mouth and the lids of her eyes drooped wearily.

A small blue vein under her right eye was swollen. There was something in a background, say what you like.

The suggestion of age and weariness in her face fascinated Mr Horsfield. It was curious to speculate about the life of a woman like that and to wonder what she appeared to herself to be – when she looked in the glass, for instance. Because, of course, she must have some pathetic illusions about herself or she would not be able to go on living. Did she still see herself young and slim, capable of anything, believing that, though every one around her grew older, she – by some miracle – remained the same? Or perhaps she was just heavily indifferent . . .

His thoughts went off at a tangent and became suddenly tinged with irritation. People ought not to look obvious; people ought to take the trouble to look and behave like all other people. And if they didn't it was their own funeral.

He said in a formal voice: 'What I meant to say was that if there is anything I can do to help you . . . '

She took out her little powder-box, opened it and looked at herself in the mirror. He went on impatiently: 'If only you'd stop worrying about how you look and tell me what's the matter.'

She said: 'I thought from the way you were staring at me that I must be looking pretty ugly.'

He felt rather ashamed, but he did not really see why he should feel ashamed.

'I didn't mean that at all,' he said.

She said: 'Oh I know, you're one of those kind blokes England is so famous for, aren't you?'

'Is England famous for kind blokes?'

'Well,' she said thoughtfully, 'that's just what England isn't famous for, really. However, kid yourself that it is. What's it got to do with me?'

'I'm all right, really,' she added, in a voice that was suddenly aloof. 'I've enough to get along with for a bit. It's simply that I wasn't able to sleep last night. The bed had a ridge right down the middle.'

Then she began to boast – boast was the only word – about some man to whom she said she had written. Apparently he had been her lover. He remembered that she had talked of the fellow when he saw her in Paris.

Mr Horsfield became rather bored. He thought that her vanity anyhow was still alive and kicking. He could not resist saying: 'I expect you have several friends in London you can write to?'

'Not me,' she said with conviction. 'I wouldn't waste three-halfpenny stamps on anybody but this man.'

Then she took a box of matches from her bag and amused herself by lighting them one after another and watching them burn down to the end. In the midst of this proceeding, she said: 'It's funny how you say one thing when you're thinking of quite another, isn't it?'

Mr Horsfield agreed.

'I must go back now,' she said. 'Truly . . . I'm pretty tired. You'll see, I shan't be like this when I've had a decent night's sleep.'

Mr Horsfield hesitated. She seemed to be waiting for something anxiously. He said: 'Well, will you dine with me next Friday?'

'Yes, I'll be very glad. I'm going to leave my hotel in a day or two, but I'll write you my new address.'

They went out and got into a taxi He thought that she was leaning very close to him. Her breath smelt of the brandy she had been drinking. He drew away.

Then he took her hand, squeezed it, and said: 'Well, on Friday then.'

A sudden stop of the taxi in a block threw her against him Her body felt soft and yielding.

'Sorry,' he said stiffly.

4

Mr Horsfield got out of the taxi with some relief. When he looked at Julia as he was saying good night he suddenly knew intimately and surely that she was perfectly indifferent to him, that the moment he had gone she would have forgotten all about him.

He said: 'Till Friday then. Good night. . . . And here! Have this to go on with.'

He had a pound-note ready folded, which he pushed into her hand.

Then he drove back to his house, which was in a small, dark street in the neighbourhood of Holland Park. Five rooms over a stable, which had been converted into a garage.

Just outside his gate a black-and-white cat sat huddled. When it saw him it opened and shut its mouth in a soundless mew.

Mr Horsfield said caressingly: 'Come along, Jones. Pretty Jones.' The cat got up, stretched slowly and, with uplifted tail, followed its master into the house.

5. Acton

The next afternoon Julia went down to the flat at Acton to see her mother.

A square of paper on which was written: OUT OF ORDER—PLEASE KNOCK, was pinned under the bell. When she had rapped twice the door opened and a boy of about sixteen stood in the dark hall staring at her.

'Is Miss Griffiths in?'

'Second floor,' said the boy. 'Oh, yes, they're in; there's always somebody there.'

The door on the second floor was opened by a middle-aged woman. Her brown hair was cut very short, drawn away from a high, narrow forehead, and brushed to lie close to her very small skull. Her nose was thin and arched. She had small, pale-brown eyes and a determined expression. She wore a coat and skirt of grey flannel, a shirt blouse, and a tie.

She said, without smiling: 'Good afternoon, Julia. Come along in.'

Julia followed her into the sitting-room.

'My name's Wyatt,' she said. 'I expect Norah's spoken about me. She'll be back in a minute or two. Have some tea.'

Her voice was casual and very agreeable.

Julia refused tea, sat down, crossed her legs, and stared downwards. She felt too nervous to talk. The meeting with her mother was very near; yet she was still unable to imagine or realize it. Supposing that her mother knew her or recognized her and with one word or glance put her outside the pale, as everybody else had done.

She felt a sort of superstitious and irrational certainty that if that happened it would finish her; it would be an ultimate and final judgement. Yet she felt cold even about this. She could not realize that it would matter.

'Can I go right in?' she said.

'She's asleep,' said Miss Wyatt. 'Just dropped off. Better not go in just yet. Norah will be back here in a minute.'

An open tin of Navy Cut tobacco and a book of cigarette-papers lay on the table near Miss Wyatt. She rolled herself a cigarette very quickly and neatly. Her gestures were like the gestures of a man. Her hands were small and thin but short-fingered and without delicacy. She said: 'Have a cigarette, Julia? There's a box of Marcovitches on the table behind you. I got them for Norah – not that she smokes much.'

Julia wanted to say: 'Please make one for me. I'd like that.' But when she met Miss Wyatt's eyes she turned without speaking, took a cigarette from the box behind her, and lit it.

'I always make my own,' Miss Wyatt said. 'I have to; it's cheaper. I started doing it a long time ago – when I was in Paris. I remember I never could stand French tobacco.'

Julia said: 'Couldn't you?'

There was a long pause.

Then Miss Wyatt began: 'In my time everybody smoked those Algerian things.' She lifted her head with an alert expression, like that of a terrier. 'There's Norah.'

Norah came in and stood by the fire, taking off her hat and coat. Her face was reddened with the cold. She seemed nervous, as though she too realized that this was a solemn and dramatic occasion. She said: 'Just a minute. I'll go in and see.'

Miss Wyatt looked at the fire without speaking. Her face had assumed a very severe expression.

Then Norah called: 'Come along in now.'

2

Julia stared at the bed and saw her mother's body – a huge, shapeless mass under the sheets and blankets – and her mother's face against the white-frilled pillow. Dark-skinned, with high cheek-bones and an aquiline nose. Her white hair, which was still long and thick, was combed into two plaits, which lay outside the sheet. One side of her face was dragged downwards. Her eyes were shut. She was breathing noisily, puffing out one corner of her mouth with each breath.

And yet the strange thing was that she was still beautiful, as an animal would be in old age.

Julia said: 'She's so much more beautiful than either of us.'

'Everybody who sees her says how nice she looks,' said Norah with pride and satisfaction in her voice. 'Would you like to sit in here for a bit? I'll go and talk to Wyatt.'

The bedroom was white-papered and comfortable. It smelt of disinfectants and eau-de-Cologne and rotten-ness.

Julia touched her mother's hand, which was lying out-side the bedclothes. Then she whispered very softly: 'Darling.' She said 'darling' with her lips, but her heart was dead.

She only knew that the room was very quiet – quiet and shut away from everything.

Curtains of thick green stuff were drawn over the windows, and the fire leaped up with small, crooked flames. A dog barked outside, far off, and somehow that made her feel happy and rested.

The things one did. Life was perfectly mad, really. And here was silence – the best thing in the world.

It seemed as if she had been sitting there for many years and that if she could go on sitting there she would learn many deep things that she had only guessed at before.

She began to whisper soundlessly: 'Oh, darling, there's something I want to explain to you. You must listen.'

Her mother's eyes opened suddenly and stared upwards. Julia put her face closer and said in a frightened, hopeful voice: 'I'm Julia, do you know? It's Julia.'

The sick woman looked steadily at her daughter. Then it was like seeing a spark go out and the eyes were again bloodshot, animal eyes. Nothing was there. She mumbled something in a thick voice, then turned her head away and began to cry, loudly and disconsolately, like a child.

Julia heard the door of the sitting-room open and Norah running along the passage.

'What is it? What is it? Is she awake?'

'She woke up suddenly. I thought she knew me just for a moment.'

'Oh, no, I shouldn't think so,' muttered Norah. 'She often cries like this.'

She took a handkerchief from under the pillow, wiped her mother's eyes and said in a crooning and mechanical voice: 'What is it, my darling? Tell me. Do you want anything? Press my hand if you want anything. . . . I expect she wants to be moved, really.'

When Julia offered to help her she answered: 'No, it's all right. The doctor showed me how to manage.'

She hauled at the inert mass, contrived to raise the head and arranged the pillows. The paralysed woman stopped crying, gave a little snort, and shut her eyes.

'She's gone to sleep again,' whispered Norah. She was breathing quickly. 'You know,' she said, 'she's a dead weight.'

They stood together at the foot of the bed.

'But I think she did know me,' persisted Julia in a whisper. 'She said something.'

'Oh, did she?'

'Yes. It sounded like "orange-trees". She must have been thinking of when she was in Brazil.'

'Oh, I daresay,' said Norah. 'You know, she called me Dobbin the other day. And I was feeling so exactly like some poor old cart-horse when she said it, too, that I simply had to laugh.'

She laughed in a high-pitched, hysterical way. Julia echoed her nervously. But when once she had begun to laugh she found it was impossible to stop herself and she went on laughing, holding on to the foot of the bed and staring at her mother.

Then she saw her mother's black eyes open again and stare back into hers with recognition and surprise and anger. They said: 'Is this why you have come back? Have you come back to laugh at me?'

Julia's heart gave a horrible leap into her throat.

She said: 'Norah, she does know me. I'm sure she does.'

The whimpering began again. Now it was louder. It was almost like a dog howling.

'Look here,' said Norah, 'you'd better go and wait in the other room for a bit.'

'Do you think I upset her?'

'Sometimes anybody strange seems to upset her. Go on; you'd better go.'

Julia went out of the room listening to Norah's crooning and authoritative voice. 'Don't cry, my darling. Don't cry, my sweet. Now, what is it? What is it you want?'

It was getting dark . . .

3

Miss Wyatt was obviously on the point of going out. She wore a macintosh. She said: 'Will you tell Norah that I'll be back before nine?'

'Yes,' said Julia. Then she said: 'Do you think my mother suffers much?'

'The doctor says she hardly suffers at all,' Miss Wyatt answered in a non-committal voice. 'Of course, she's got worse lately. She's undoubtedly worse. Norah had to sit up with her every night last week. I haven't liked the look of her at all this last day or two.

'Norah's a good kid,' added Miss Wyatt. 'She's had a long time of this and I've never heard her grouse, never once. She's a good kid. And she'll be all right. She'll be all right. She's young yet.'

When Miss Wyatt had gone Julia put her hands over her ears to shut out the cries from the next room, which had grown louder and more pitiful. Then they stopped abruptly. Julia took a deep breath, got a handkerchief out of her bag, and wiped her hands.

Norah came in almost at once. She said: 'Where's Wyatt?'

'Gone out. She said she'd be back before nine. Has she gone to sleep?'

Norah nodded.

'But it's horrible,' muttered Julia. 'Horrible.'

'Yes,' answered Norah. 'It is. . . . Let's make some more tea, shall we? Or, wait a minute, will you have some vermouth? Wyatt brought me a bottle the other day.'

She found the bottle, filled two glasses, and drank her own quickly. Then she said in a voice that sounded defiant: 'I expect you find all this very sordid and ugly, don't you?'

Julia said: 'No, no.' But she stopped because she was unable to put her emotion into words. At that moment her sister seemed to her like a character in a tremendous tragedy moving, dark, tranquil, and beautiful, across a background of yellowish snow.

'Not a bit,' she said.

They did not speak for some seconds; then Norah said with a half-laugh: 'Well, we've neither of us done very well for ourselves, have we?'

Julia lifted her shoulders, as if to say: 'Well, don't ask me.'

'The fact is,' said Norah, 'that there's something wrong with our family. We're soft, or lazy, or something.'

'I don't think you are lazy,' said Julia. 'And I shouldn't say that you were too soft, either.'

She spoke gently, but Norah felt suddenly breathless, as if they were on the verge of a quarrel. She muttered: 'No, I don't think I'm soft now. . . . Perhaps I'm not very soft now.'

She felt a tightness of the throat, and her eyes stung. She opened them widely, and leaned her head back, because she knew that if she did that the tears would not fall; they would go back to wherever they came from. She did not want to give herself away before Julia – Julia with her hateful, blackened eyelids. What was the use of telling Julia what she thought of her? It was ridiculous to make a scene. You ignored people like that.

And yet every time she looked at Julia she felt a fierce desire to hurt her or to see her hurt and humiliated. She thought in a confused way, 'It's because I'm so tired.' All day she had felt like that, as if she could not bear another instant. When she had held a spoon of medicine to her mother's lips her hands had shaken so violently that it had all been spilled. And all last night she had lain awake thinking, instead of sleeping, now that Wyatt was there, and she had a chance to sleep. She had lain awake thinking and crying – and to cry was a thing she hardly ever did.

It was as if meeting Julia had aroused some spirit of rebellion to tear her to bits. She thought over and over again, 'It isn't fair, it isn't fair.'

She picked up the book lying on her bed-table – *Almayer's Folly* – and had begun to read:

The slave had no hope, and knew of no change. She knew of no other sky, no other water, no other forest, no other world, no other life. She had no wish, no hope, no love. . . . The absence of pain and hunger was her happiness, and when she felt unhappy she was tired, more than usual, after the day's labour.

Then she had got up and looked at herself in the glass. She had let her nightgown slip down off her shoulders, and had a look at herself. She was tall and straight and slim and young – well, fairly young. She had taken up a strand of her hair and put her face against it and thought how she liked the smell and the feel of it. She had laughed at herself in the glass and her teeth were white and sound and even. Yes, she had laughed at herself in the glass. Like an idiot.

Then in the midst of her laughter she had noticed how pale her lips were; and she had thought: 'My life's like death. It's like being buried alive. It isn't fair, it isn't fair.'

She could not stop crying. It had been as if something terribly strong were struggling within her, and tearing her in its struggles. And then she had thought: 'If this goes on for another year I'm finished. I'll be old and finished, and that's that.'

Of course, she had thought that sort of thing before. But always vaguely – and there had not been anything vague about the way she had thought last night.

Everybody always said to her: 'You're wonderful, Norah, you're wonderful. I don't know how you do it.' It was a sort of drug, that universal, that unvarying admiration – the feeling that one was doing what one ought to do, the approval of God and man. It made you feel protected and safe, as if something very powerful were fighting on your side.

Besides, she wasn't a squeamish sort. She could bear disgusting sights and sounds and smells. And so she had slaved. And she had gradually given up going out because she was too tired to try to amuse herself. Besides, there wasn't any money.

That had gone on for six years. Three years ago her mother had had a second stroke, and since then her life had been slavery.

Everybody had said: 'You're wonderful, Norah.' But they did not help. They just stood around watching her youth die, and her beauty die, and her soft heart grow hard and bitter. They sat there and said: 'You're wonderful, Norah.' Beasts. . . . Devils . . .

For a long time she had just lain on her bed, thinking: 'Beasts and devils.' And then gradually she had begun to think: 'No, that isn't fair.' They were not beasts. They approved, and were willing to back their approval, but not in any spectacular fashion. And then she had begun to think – in a dull, sore sort of manner – about Aunt Sophie's will, and the will her mother had made. And that at long last she would have some money of her own and be able to do what she liked.

And then she had felt very cold, and had pulled the bedclothes over her. And then she had felt so tired that after all nothing mattered except sleep. And then she must have slept.

Julia moved; she uncrossed her legs. She had been thinking of the words 'Orange-trees', remembering the time when she had woven innumerable romances about her mother's childhood in South America, when she had asked innumerable questions, which her mother had answered inadequately or not at all, for she was an inarticulate woman. Natural, accepting transplantation as a plant might have done. But sometimes you could tell that she was sickening for the sun. Julia remembered her saying: 'This is a cold, grey country. This isn't a country to be really happy in.' Had she then been unhappy? No, Julia did not remember her as an unhappy woman. Austere, unconsciously thwarted perhaps, but not unhappy.

She said, in a diffident voice: 'Can I come again tomorrow?'

'Of course,' Norah said. And then: 'Have something to

eat before you go. Bread and cheese, or an egg, or something.'

'No, thank you,' said Julia. 'No, thank you. Don't bother.'

'I'll come to the door with you,' said Norah. She now felt that she did not want to let Julia go. She hated her, but she felt more alive when her sister was with her.

Outside, the sky was clear and pale blue. There was a thin young moon, red-gold.

'Look,' said Julia. 'New moon.'

Norah suddenly began to shiver violently. Julia could see her teeth chattering. She said: 'Till tomorrow, then,' and went in and shut the door.

4

On the next day, which was a Sunday, Julia went down to Acton and sat for an hour in her mother's room.

This time the sick woman lay like a log, without moving, without opening her eyes.

Julia sat there remembering that when she was a very young child she had loved her mother. Her mother had been the warm centre of the world. You loved to watch her brushing her long hair; and when you missed the caresses and the warmth you groped for them. . . And then her mother – entirely wrapped up in the new baby – had said things like, 'Don't be a cry-baby. You're too old to go on like that. You're a great big girl of six.' And from being the warm centre of the world her mother had gradually become a dark, austere, rather plump woman, who, because she was worried, slapped you for no reason that you knew. So that there were times when you were afraid of her; other times when you disliked her.

Then you stopped being afraid or disliking. You simply became indifferent and tolerant and rather sentimental, because after all she was your mother.

It was strange sitting there, and remembering the time

when she was the sweet, warm centre of the world, remembering it so vividly that mysteriously it was all there again.

When it began to grow dark she went back into the sitting-room.

Miss Wyatt asked: 'Are you going?'

'Is there nothing I can do?' said Julia.

'No,' said Miss Wyatt. 'Norah will be back very soon.'

Then she began to read again, because she did not like, approve of, or even trust the creature and she made no bones about showing it.

Julia felt herself dismissed. After fidgeting about a little, she said: 'Well, good night.'

'Good night,' said Miss Wyatt, without looking up. 'Are you coming here tomorrow?'

'I don't know,' said Julia in a low voice. 'Yes, I think I will. . . . But I don't know, because I'm changing my room. Here's my new address. Will you give it to Norah?'

On her return to the hotel the young man at the reception desk presented her with a bit of paper.

'A telephone message for you, madam.'

Julia read:

'Mr James says he will be pleased to see Madame Martin either tonight or tomorrow night between nine and ten if she will call round at his house.'

6. Mr James

This was the affair which had ended quietly and decently, without fuss or scenes or hysteria. When you were nineteen, and it was the first time you had been let down, you did not make scenes. You felt as if your back was broken, as if you would never move again. But you did not make a scene. That started later on, when the same thing had happened five or six times over, and you were supposed to be getting used to it.

Nineteen – that was a hell of a long time ago. Well, you had your reward, because there was a man who had become your friend for life. Always at the back of your mind had been the thought: 'If the worst absolutely comes to the worst he'll help.'

He had said: 'I am your friend for life. I am eternally grateful to you – for your sweetness and your generosity.' And so on and so on.

He was *chic*, too. He had lent her a good deal of money, first and last. And she had always said: 'This money I have borrowed. I will pay you back one day.'

And then he would reply: 'Of course you will. Don't you worry about that.'

And after all this time he had answered almost at once. That was *chic*.

2

The servant who opened the door had a nice face – not the sort that sneered at you after your back was turned. There was a big wood fire burning in the hall, and a lot of comfortable chairs.

Then the servant showed her upstairs and opened the door of a room, and there he was.

Another person. Nothing to be nervous about or sentimental about. This was simply another person – just as she was another person. That was strange and rather sad.

Then she began thinking that it must be strange to be very rich and absolutely secure, and not stupid. Because so many very rich people were stupid; only half their brains worked. 'But after all, perhaps he is stupid,' she thought. 'I don't really know'

'My dear, I'm awfully glad to see you. You were a dear to write.'

He was thinking: 'These resurrections of the past are tactless, really – not amusing. But what is one to do?'

He had the beginnings of a headache – the faint throb-bings in the temples.

Julia said, with a coquettish expression: 'Well, d'you think I've changed?'

He reassured her. 'You've never looked prettier. Never prettier.'

'Not too fat?' she said anxiously.

He said: 'Just exactly right,' and smiled at her.

But she felt a little as though she were sitting in an office waiting for an important person who might do something for her – or might not. And when she looked round the room it seemed to her a very beautiful room, and she felt that she had no right to sit there and intrude her sordid wish somehow to keep alive into that beautiful room.

Then he said, trying to be kind: 'Look here, you can tell me all about it, because I've got loads of time – heaps of time. Nearly three-quarters of an hour.'

She thought that she must start the explanation she had prepared. She said, as one would say something off by heart: 'I tried, you know, to make things a success after I married, but I didn't pull it off. It fell through.'

'Yes, I gathered that when I saw you last. I'm sorry for it.'

'And then, you see, when he didn't really care any more it seemed natural to leave him.'

'And there was somebody else who did care, or said he did? Was that it?'

'Oh, not particularly,' she said. 'After a time there was somebody, but that was never the real reason. It was just that everything had gone wrong and he seemed fed up and I felt it was natural to go away if he was like that.'

'I see,' said Mr James.

She was thinking: 'It was just my luck, wasn't it, that when we needed it most we should have lost everything? When you've just had a baby, and it dies for the simple reason that you haven't enough money to keep it alive, it leaves you with a sort of hunger. Not sentimental – oh, no. Just a funny feeling, like hunger. And then, of course, you're indifferent – because the whole damned thing is too stupid to be anything else but indifferent about. . . . He's so little. And he dies and is put under the earth.'

She looked at Mr James, his slightly puckered forehead and the carefully kind expression on his face.

'And then you rush round trying to raise money enough to bury him. You don't want to leave him lying in the hospital with a card tied round his wrist. And the tart downstairs lends money and buys flowers and comes to see you and cries because you are crying. "Look here, I don't believe that; you're making it up." All right, don't believe it then.'

And there was Neil James puckering his forehead, trying to be so kind. So kind, so cautious, so perfectly certain that all is for the best and that no mistakes are ever made.

'How rum if after all these years I hated him – not for any reason except that he's so damned respectable and secure. Sitting there so smugly.'

Mr James looked at her, rather uneasy at her long silence, and said: 'Look here, have a whisky-and-soda.'

He rang the bell and, when the servant arrived, said: 'Bring whisky and glasses.'

'Well,' she said slowly, 'I've been all right really, as a matter of fact.'

Mr James glanced sideways at the clock.

'But you want to go out,' she said. 'I'm keeping you.'

'For god's sake sit still, there's heaps of time.'

So many threads. To try to disentangle them – no use. Because he has money he's a kind of god. Because I have none I'm a kind of worm. A worm because I've failed and I have no money. A worm because I'm not even sure if I hate you.

She said, rather sullenly: 'I got fed up. I felt I needed a rest. I thought perhaps you'd help me to have a rest.'

At last she has come to the point – relief of Mr James! And yet he felt harder, now that he was sure she had come to ask for money. Everybody tried to get money out of him. By God, he was sick of it. 'If I don't look out this is never going to stop; it's going to be an unending business.'

A suspicion came into his mind. He asked, even as Uncle Griffiths had done: 'And you don't know where your husband is?'

She looked at him with a bewildered expression and shook her head.

'Of course, my dear,' he said, 'I'll do something for you. Look here. I'll write you tomorrow and send you something. Don't worry, I won't forget. I promise. You'll be able to have a rest. . . . Now let's talk about something else for God's sake.'

She said, rather stubbornly: 'But I always meant, when I saw you, to explain. . . . '

Mr James said: 'My dear, don't harrow me. I don't want to hear. Let's talk about something else.'

Then, when the man had brought the whisky and retired, he said: 'There's your whisky. Go on, drink it up.'

For the first time she looked straight into his eyes. She said: 'My dear, I wouldn't harrow you for the world. "No harrowing" is my motto.'

She drank the whisky. Gaiety spread through her. Why care a damn?

She said: 'Look here, why talk about harrowing? Harrowing doesn't come into it. I've had good times – lots of good times.'

She thought: 'I had a shot at the life I wanted. And I failed. . . . All right! I might have succeeded, and if I had people would have licked my boots for me. There wouldn't have been any of this cold-shouldering. Don't tell me; leave me alone. If I hate, I've a right to hate. And if I think people are swine, let me think it. . . . '

She said: 'Anyhow, I don't know how I could have done differently. I wish I'd been cleverer about it, that's all. Do you think I could have done differently?'

He looked away from her, and said: 'Don't ask me. I'm not the person to ask that sort of thing, am I? I don't know. Probably you couldn't. You know, Julietta, the war taught me a lot.'

'Did it?' she said, surprised. 'Did it though?'

'Yes. Before the war I'd always thought that I rather despised people who didn't get on.'

'Despised,' thought Julia. 'Why despised?'

'I despised a man who didn't get on. I didn't believe much in bad luck. But after the war I felt differently. I've got a lot of mad friends now. I call them my mad friends.'

'People who haven't got on?' Julia asked.

'Yes. People who've come croppers.'

'Men?'

'Oh, no, some women too. Though mind you, women are a different thing altogether. Because it's all nonsense; the life of a man and the life of a woman can't be compared. They're up against entirely different things the whole time. What's the use of talking nonsense about it? Look at cocks and hens; it's the same sort of thing,' said Mr James.

Then he said: 'Look here, Julietta, before you go you must come and look at my pictures.'

3

When they looked at the pictures he became a different man. Because he loved them he became in their presence modest, hesitating, unsure of his own opinion.

'Do you like that?'

'Yes, I like it.'

'I wish I could get somebody who knows to tell me whether it's any good or not,' he said, talking to himself.

He was anxious because he did not want to love the wrong thing. Fancy wanting to be told what you must love!

'Well, look here, Julietta, good-bye. Don't worry. I'll write at once; you shall have your rest. And let me know your address when you go back to Paris.'

'Yes,' she said, 'I will. And I'm at another place here. I'll write it down for you.' She got an envelope and a stump of pencil out of her bag, wrote on it and gave it to him.

'All right, all right,' said Mr James, putting it into his pocket without looking at it. 'I won't forget.'

She wanted to cry as he went down the stairs with her. There was a lump in her throat. She thought: 'That wasn't what I wanted.' She had hoped that he would say something or look something that would make her feel less lonely.

There was a vase of flame-coloured tulips in the hall – surely the most graceful of flowers. Some thrust their heads forward like snakes, and some were very erect, stiff, virginal, rather prim. Some were dying, with curved grace in their death.

7. Change of Address

The next day Julia did not go down to Acton. She walked all the afternoon in a pale sunlight – sunlight without warmth. She did not think, because a spell was on her that forbade her to think. She walked with her eyes on the ground, and a puff of wind blew capriciously before her a little piece of greasy brown paper, omnibus tickets, a torn newspaper poster, coal dust, and dried horse dung.

These streets near her boarding-house on Notting Hill seemed strangely empty, like the streets of a grey dream – a labyrinth of streets, all exactly alike.

She would think: 'Surely I passed down here several minutes ago.' Then she would see the name Chepstow Crescent or Pembridge Villas, and reassure herself. 'That's all right; I'm not walking in a circle.'

At last she got on a bus and went to a cinema in the Edgware Road. A comic film was going on, and a woman behind her laughed, 'Heh, heh, heh.' A fat, comfortable laugh, pleasant to listen to, so that without looking round she could tell what the woman was like.

After the comedy she saw young men running races and some of them collapsing exhausted. And then – strange anti-climax – young women ran races and also collapsed exhausted, at which the audience rocked with laughter.

She came out of the cinema at nine o'clock, ate something at a Lyons' tea-shop, went back to her bedroom, and slept.

2

Somebody was knocking at the door.

Julia called out sleepily: '*Entrez*. . . . Come in.'

The knocking went on and she shrieked, sitting up in bed: 'Come in, I said.'

A yellow-haired maid advanced one pace into the room and said in a detached manner: 'You're wanted on the telephone, miss.'

'What?. . . Yes, I'm coming, I'm coming.'

Her slippers were by the bedside. She could not see her dressing-gown. She could not remember where she had put it. It didn't matter.

Outside on the landing a gust from the open window cut through her thin pyjamas. She put up her hand to shield her chest and rushed past the maid. Her hair stood wildly up around her head. Her eyes were dark with last night's make-up, which she had been too tired to take off.

The maid thought: 'Tart.'

'Is that Mrs Martin? Miss Griffiths says, will you come as quickly as possible. Mrs Griffiths is very bad. As quickly as possible.'

'Yes,' said Julia to the telephone. 'Yes. At once. In three-quarters of an hour, say.'

As she mounted the stairs she was filled with a sort of helpless terror at the thought of the time that must elapse before she reached Acton and of the innumerable details that must fill up that time. She was thinking as she ran up the stairs: 'I'll never do it, never. Oh God, all the things I'll have to do before I'm there!'

Her legs were weak.

In seven minutes she was ready, but when she looked in the glass she thought that she had never seen herself looking quite so ugly. It would be a kind of disrespect to go like that. She took her hat off and sponged her face with cold water, powdered it, brushed her hair flat and pulled out her side-locks carefully from under her hat.

All the time she was doing this, something in her brain was saying coldly and clearly: 'Hurry, monkey, hurry. This is death. Death doesn't wait. Hurry, monkey, hurry.'

She walked along the street wondering whether she should take a taxi and ask Norah to pay for it. She was still arguing the matter to herself when she reached the Tube station. She had imagined that it was very early in the morning, but when she looked at the clock she found that it was a quarter to ten.

The girl standing next to her in the lift stared at her persistently. She grew angry and thought: 'Well, I can stare too, if it comes to that.' She narrowed her eyes and glared. The girl was short and slim. She had a round face, round brown eyes, a small nose, and a small round hat. She wore a tight-waisted coat trimmed with fur and her gloveless hands, protruding thick and red from her coat sleeves, grasped a patent leather bag. Some fool probably thought her pretty. Some male fool-counterpart with round eyes and a little button mouth.

When she realized that Julia was staring at her she coughed, drew her lips down, and turned her back. 'Bad luck to you then,' thought Julia. 'Bad luck to you.'

The lift gates slid open. . . .

When Julia was sitting in the train she stopped thinking of the people around. She became calm.

8. Death

Norah opened the door. She wore her green dress with the red rose sewn on the shoulder. They went along the dark passage. Julia was frightened. She was also intensely curious.

But when she saw her mother she forgot herself and began to cry from pity.

Her mother's face was white and sunken in and covered with sweat. She was fighting hard for every breath, and every breath seemed to be a torture. 'She can't breathe again,' Julia thought. 'That must be the last time.'

But still she fought. A strong woman.

Norah sat on a wicker chair near the bedside. Beyond her tears and fright she was thinking: 'I did all I could. I did all I could.' She had a handkerchief in her hand and every now and then she leant forward and wiped her mother's face with a grave gesture, as if she were accomplishing a rite. Something in the poise of her body and in her serene face was old, old, old.

The blinds were half-lowered in the room. A nurse sat at the back. She was a fat blonde. Norah whispered: 'Yesterday afternoon, when nurse came, she thought it was only a matter of a few hours. And when the doctor came this morning, he said: "An hour or so." '

The nurse leaned forward and whispered rather fussily to Julia: 'You mustn't be too distressed, my dear, because your mother is not suffering. She isn't conscious. She isn't suffering at all.'

'Oh, isn't she?' said Julia. She thought: 'I must pray. It's probably no good, but somebody must try. It might be some good.'

She shut her eyes on the twilight of the room and began to mutter:

Eternal rest give unto her, O Lord.
Let perpetual light shine upon her.
May she rest in peace.

Her lips were dry. She moistened them and went on praying.

Norah was whispering: 'Would you like something to eat?'

'No.'

'Some tea? Jane's in the kitchen; she'll make you some.'

'No,' Julia whispered. 'I'm not hungry. Really.'

Norah got up and went and spoke in a low voice to the nurse. She was saying: 'Go and have something to eat – or some tea,' and the nurse was answering: 'No, my dear, no.'

That again was as if she were following a ritual, because death and eating were connected.

But after that Julia stopped praying. She could think no more than 'If she could only die. . . . If she could only die. She must be suffering.'

2

It was nearly two o'clock when the sick woman gave a groan. The nurse got up. 'Call Miss Wyatt,' she said.

And then Miss Wyatt was standing there too. Standing as if she were waiting for something to happen. Everyone stood waiting for something to happen.

The dying woman breathed three times gently, without any effort. Her head dropped sideways.

'She's gone,' said the nurse. She stopped crying and her expression became professional.

'Gone.' That was the word. Norah bent down, weeping, and kissed her mother's forehead. Then she drew aside and looked at her sister. In her turn Julia bent for the ritual kiss – rather awkwardly. She thought that they were all looking at her, expecting perhaps some violent and hysterical outburst.

Miss Wyatt had her hand on Norah's shoulder. Julia

trailed after them into the sitting-room, which looked very bright and cheerful. Through the glass door one could see the thin branches of a solitary tree against the cold grey sky. Her mother had said: 'I can't rest in this country. This is such a cold, grey country.'

Suddenly Julia thought: 'All the same, we have left her just when she wants us.' She got up to go back into the bedroom, but her legs felt weak.

Miss Wyatt was patting her on the shoulder. 'Cheer up, Julia,' she said.

The pretty little maid came in with tea and bread-and-butter. She also was crying, but one could see that the excitement was not altogether unpleasant to her.

The tea tasted good. Suddenly there was a feeling of rest and relaxation in the room. 'That's over. Life is sweet.'

'Just a minute,' muttered Julia. The feeling that her mother needed her urgently was too strong. It forced her out of the room.

When she turned the handle of the bedroom door the nurse's fussy voice called: 'What is it?'

'Can I come in, nurse, just for a minute?'

'No, not now. I'll call you when you can come. Not now.'

Julia went back into the sitting-room and drank some more tea. Nobody spoke. Every now and then Norah would begin to cry gently; and then she would wipe her face and blow her nose and sit motionless again, her head bent.

At about five o'clock the nurse knocked at the door and called Norah. There was a lot of whispering in the passage and then, after a while, the nurse put her head in again and called Julia. She followed the other woman into the bedroom. Contrary to what she imagined, it felt empty, and she was bewildered, as though some comfort that she had thought she would find there had failed her.

'Doesn't she look lovely?' said the nurse.

But Julia thought that her mother's sunken face, bound with white linen, looked frightening – horribly frightening, like a mask. Always masks had frightened and fascinated her.

She forced herself to stoop and kiss the dead woman.

Norah put her hand out and squeezed her sister's arm. Norah was very tired and sad, but behind her sadness was a rested feeling which made her feel gentle and pitiful to everyone, even for the moment to Julia. It was as if the hard core of her heart was melted.

When they got out of the bedroom she said very gently: 'Sure you're all right, Julia?'

'Oh, yes,' said Julia. She was all right. She was only very sleepy, horribly sleepy, as a child would be after a very exciting day.

3

Out in the street Julia thought suddenly, 'I must look ghastly.'

She stood under a lamp-post and powdered her face, and pulled her hat over her eyes. 'It seems a year since last night,' she thought.

There was a barrel-organ playing at the corner of the street, and that made her want to cry again. To its jerky tune she tried to set words:

> Go rolling down to Rio
> (Roll down – roll down to Rio!)
> And I'd like to roll to Rio
> Some day before I'm old!

All the way home she was thinking: 'If I have any luck, I oughtn't to meet anybody on the stairs. They all ought to be eating just now.'

She opened the door of her boarding-house very gently and cautiously. On the fifth landing the door opposite her bedroom opened, and her neighbour, who was a small, thin woman, with dark hair, put her head out.

'Good evening,' she said.

'Good evening,' said Julia.

'Aren't you going down to dinner?'

Julia shook her head. She was suddenly unable to speak.

'Well, won't you have some tea?' said the woman, staring at her with curiosity. 'I'm just making myself a cup.'

'No,' answered Julia. 'No, thank you.' She went quickly into her bedroom, and locked the door.

As soon as she was alone the desire to cry left her again, and she was filled with only one wish – a longing for sleep. The stupid thing was that the barrel-organ tune was still ringing in her head, and she could not quite fit the words to it:

> Yes, weekly from Southampton,
> Great steamers, white and gold,
> Go rolling down to Rio
> (Roll down – roll down to Rio!)
> And I'd like to roll to Rio
> Some day before I'm old.

9. Golders Green

Julia said: 'How much are these roses?'

'Six shillings the bunch, madam. Roses are expensive at this time of the year,' said the florist.

They were red roses, but frail and drooping, with very long, thin stalks. They would not last long.

Julia thought: 'Poor devils, poor devils, what a fate for them!' But she remembered that she had determined the day before to buy roses for her mother.

'Give me that bunch,' she said. She took her last ten-shilling note from her bag.

When she arrived in the afternoon carrying the roses, Norah was fussing about the death certificate, which she thought she had lost. 'Where is it? I know I put it down somewhere.'

'Oh, it'll turn up. Don't get in a state,' said Miss Wyatt.

Julia sat silently by the fire. She looked ill. Norah thought she had a lost expression, but Norah was too busy to think about that. She came in to ask: 'Look here, Julia, do you think we ought to have the choir?'

'No,' said Julia. 'Why?'

Norah said: 'I think she'd have liked it.'

'Oh, well, have it then, have it.'

'It's that I have so little ready money,' said Norah unhappily. 'I'm so afraid of running short.'

It was decided at last they should have the organist, but no choir. The choir was a luxury they could not afford. And then they decided that Chopin was preferable to the *Dead March* in *Saul*. And then Julia said she must go, that she was horribly tired, that she had not slept, that she must go home.

'Are you coming tomorrow?'

'No,' said Julia. 'At least, I'm not sure.'

'Well, you'll be here on Friday,' persisted Norah. 'Friday at nine o'clock.'

'Oh, yes, rather,' said Julia. 'Of course.'

She turned at the door to say: 'Those roses. Put them in water, will you? Not – not inside.'

2

On the Friday morning at nine o'clock, everybody was thinking: 'Why don't we start?'

'We are waiting for Julia,' Norah whispered to Uncle Griffiths at last.

'Well, I shouldn't wait an indefinite time if I were you,' he whispered back. 'Not an indefinite time.'

Norah thought miserably: 'I knew there'd be a hitch.'

Her heart was beating with nervousness. She felt that her sister's absence would be an unbearable calamity, a disgrace, the last straw. When the bell rang, she was so relieved that she forgot to be annoyed.

Julia said: 'I'm sorry; I couldn't help it.'

They went together into the sitting-room, where there were two women whom Julia did not know.

A fussy voice called: 'Ladies for the first carriage, please.' And then: 'Ladies for the second carriage.'

With solemn faces everyone trooped out of the front door to the two waiting cars.

In the first car Norah and Julia sat side by side. Miss Wyatt and Uncle Griffiths faced them. Julia sat sideways, so that her knees should not touch her uncle's knees. He gave her one disapproving, almost furtive look, then turned his head away and looked out of the window. He was spick and span, solemn and decorous, but he felt old and very melancholy that morning.

He thought how he disliked that woman and her expression, and her eyes, which said: 'Oh, for God's sake, leave me alone. I'm not troubling you; you've no right to trouble me. I've as much right as you to live, haven't I?' But you were sure that, underneath that expression, people like her were preparing the filthy abuse they would use, the dirty tricks they would try to play, if they imagined you were not leaving them alone.

3

It was a mild day. The sky was the rare, hazy, and tender blue of the London sky in spring. There was such sweetness in the air that it benumbed you. It woke up in you a hope that was a stealthy pain.

Julia watched the shadows as they passed – the angular shadows of houses and the dark, slender shadows of the leafless branches, like an uneven row of dancers in the position 'Arabesque'.

She heard Uncle Griffiths saying: 'Oh, yes, these people must have the best of everything nowadays. The best meat, the best butter . . .'

Norah was silent, looking down at her hands clasped together in her lap.

4

The car stopped. Everybody walked in a short procession up to the chapel of the Crematorium, where a clergyman with very bright blue eyes was waiting. That was a dream, too, but a painful dream, because she was obsessed with the feeling that she was so close to seeing the thing that was behind all this talking and posturing, and that the talking and the posturing were there to prevent her from seeing it. Now it's time to get up; now it's time to kneel down; now it's time to stand up.

But all the time she stood, knelt, and listened she was tortured because her brain was making a huge effort to grapple with nothingness. And the effort hurt; yet it was almost successful. In another minute she would know. And then a dam inside her head burst, and she leant her head on her arms and sobbed.

The coffin slid forward in a slow and very stealthy manner. Norah watched it with eyes wide open. Her hands were clutching at the back of the pew in front of her. She glanced sideways at Uncle Griffiths. He looked frightened. Yes, there was a look of fear in his eyes. She thought: 'Poor old boy.'

The thing was going so slowly. She shut her eyes and tried to pray, but she could not. They managed it all very well, very well indeed. The word slick came into her mind. Slick.

Julia had abandoned herself. She was kneeling and sobbing and wishing she had brought another handkerchief. She was crying now because she remembered that her life had been a long succéssion of humiliations and mistakes and pains and ridiculous efforts. Everybody's life was like that. At the same time, in a miraculous manner, some essence of her was shooting upwards like a flame. She was great. She was a defiant flame shooting upwards not to

94

plead but to threaten. Then the flame sank down again, useless, having reached nothing.

She sat up and blinked. Her arm had been pressed over her eyes so tightly that she could not see. Norah was not there; she had followed the parson somewhere. Uncle Griffiths had retired to the farthest end of the pew.

They were all standing on a wide portico at the back of the chapel. A wide portico. A lot of flowers. And then an open space spotted with sunlight.

When you cried like that it made you feel childish. You could be comforted quite childishly. 'Of course,' she thought, 'Heaven. Naturally. I daresay all this is a lot of fuss about nothing.'

Miss Wyatt came up and took her arm. She said: 'Come along now, Julia, come along.'

They were seated in the car. It was all over. Life was sweet and truly a pleasant thing.

Norah said: 'Are you coming back to lunch, Uncle Griffiths?'

And Uncle Griffiths answered that he didn't mind if he did.

5

During luncheon Uncle Griffiths talked about pickpockets. He told them that he had discovered, or had been informed, that the best pickpockets wore false arms which they kept ostentatiously folded over their chests while the real ones did the job. He told a long story about a pickpocket with false arms whom he had met in a lift. 'But I spotted the chap at once.'

Somebody said: 'And did he pick your pocket?'

Uncle Griffiths said: 'I didn't give him the chance.'

'Poor man!' murmured Miss Wyatt. 'After taking all that trouble. Let's hope he managed to pick somebody's.'

Everybody laughed.

The french window into the little garden was open. The

room was full of sunlight subdued to a grey glare and then suddenly of shadows. 'Life is sweet and truly a pleasant thing.'

Norah sat with her shoulders bowed a little, as though both the effort and the relief were over and she faced a certain blankness.

When luncheon was over, Uncle Griffiths sat in the arm-chair and went on talking, eagerly, as if the sound of his own voice laying down the law to his audience of females reassured him. He talked and talked. He talked about life, about literature, about Dostoievsky.

He said: 'Why see the world through the eyes of an epileptic?'

Julia spoke mechanically, as one's foot shoots out when a certain nerve in the knee is struck: 'But he might see things very clearly, mightn't he? At moments.'

'Clearly?' said Uncle Griffiths. 'Why clearly? How d'you mean clearly?'

Nobody answered.

Norah said: 'Julia, will you come out here for a minute? I want to talk to you.'

6

The blinds were still drawn in the bedroom where their mother had lain, and the room was dark and cold and very empty. It smelt, faintly, of roses, and another smell, musty and rotten.

Norah said: 'I wanted to give you this.' She handed her sister a thin gold ring with a red stone in it. 'She'd have liked you to have something.'

'Oh, thank you,' said Julia. Her eyes were fixed on the bed.

Norah said in a confidential voice, averting her eyes: 'I've decided to leave London at once. I'm going to shut this place up. You know, I feel rather awful now it's all over. Wyatt's coming with me. I hope to get away the day after tomorrow. Write and tell me how you get on, won't you?'

Julia made an assenting noise. She sat huddled up. Her nose shone brightly through an inadequate coating of powder. She looked ugly and dazed.

Norah said: 'And look here; don't ever pawn that ring. If you're on the verge of pawning it, send it back to me and I'll always give you a pound for it.'

'Oh, I won't do that,' said Julia in a hostile voice.

Then she said: 'I've managed to borrow something from that man I told you about. And that's pretty lucky for me, isn't it?'

She stopped. There was nothing more to be said, but neither of them made any movement to go. Norah stood near the door. When she looked at her sister her eyes were inquisitive. They were inquisitive, and there was a yellow flicker in them.

She said: 'I'm sorry that you were so upset today, but I can understand that you feel miserable. Sorry for everything.'

Julia said: 'Sorry? But it was rage. Didn't you understand that? Don't you know the difference between sorrow and rage?'

'Rage? Why rage?' said Norah sharply.

'Oh, it doesn't matter,' muttered Julia. 'This isn't the time to talk about it, anyway.'

Her hands were very cold and she rubbed them together in her lap.

'But I think it is the time to talk about it,' persisted Norah. Then the thought came to her: 'Now then, that's enough. Stop it. Leave her alone.'

Yet she went on in a cold voice: 'How do you mean rage?'

Julia said: 'Animals are better than we are, aren't they? They're not all the time pretending and lying and sneering, like loathsome human beings.'

'You're an extraordinary creature,' said Norah. She enjoyed seeing her sister grow red and angry, and begin to talk in an incoherent voice.

Julia talked on and on, answering the yellow gleam of cruelty in Norah's eyes.

'People are such beasts, such mean beasts,' she said. 'They'll let you die for want of a decent word, and then they'll lick the feet of anybody they can get anything out of. And do you think I'm going to cringe to a lot of mean, stupid animals? If all good, respectable people had one face, I'd spit in it. I wish they all had one face so that I could spit in it.'

'You mean all that for me, I suppose,' said Norah. She spoke calmly, but she felt very giddy. Now the blood ran up to her own face. There was tingling in her finger-tips. She thought: 'She's disgusting, that's what she is. She's my sister, and she's disgusting.'

Julia said in a sullen voice: 'Mean it for you? I don't know. Perhaps I do.' She saw before her a huge, stupid face. 'Spit in it,' she thought. 'Spit in it once before I die.' She clutched her hands, and made a grimace.

Norah said: 'Perhaps if I were to start telling you my opinion of you, I'd have something to say too. After the way you've gone on.' She thought: 'Now then, hold on. Shut up.'

'You don't know anything about the way I've gone on,' said Julia. 'Not a thing. What do you know about me, or care? Not a damn thing. Listen! When I saw that you'd changed and that you looked older, as if you'd had a rotten time, I cried, d'you see? I cried about you. Have you ever cried one tear for me? You've never once looked at me as if you cared whether I lived or died. And you think I don't know why? It's because you're jealous. That's the bedrock. All you people who've knuckled under – you're jealous. D'you think I don't know? You're jealous of me, jealous, jealous. Eaten up with it.'

Norah's face went dusky-red, then white. She lifted her hand threateningly.

'Jealous,' screamed Julia. Then a horrible spasm of pity shot through her because her sister's face was so white – white, with bluish lips.

Norah opened the door, and ran along the passage, sobbing loudly. She went into the sitting-room and shut the door after her. Julia, following her, heard her talking and making sobbing explanations, and she began to shout some incoherent defence of herself through the door. 'I didn't start it. I didn't start it.'

The door of the sitting-room opened, and Uncle Griffiths appeared. He said: 'Will you stop making that noise? It's disgraceful; it's unheard of. Today of all days. You've forgotten how to behave yourself among respectable people. This,' said Uncle Griffiths with emphasis, 'is not a bad house.'

'You're an abominable old man,' said Julia.

Uncle Griffiths made a rapid and dignified movement backwards, and shut the door in her face.

She stood for a second or two outside it, listening to Norah sobbing and talking at the same time. Then she went back into the bedroom. And suddenly she was immensely calm and indifferent to anything that had ever happened or could possibly happen to her. It was like that. Just when in another moment your brain would burst, it was always like that. She sat placidly with her knees rather wide apart, and her eyes fixed calm.

She felt nothing, except that she was tired and that she wished to be left alone to rest there, quietly, in the darkened room. It seemed to her that she had been there for ever and that she always would be there, and that getting up, moving, would be impossible. But they must leave her alone, leave her alone. Then even that thought left her. She floated . . . floated. . . . And shut her eyes.

She heard someone go along the passage. The front door shut. Then, almost immediately, Miss Wyatt came in.

Miss Wyatt said in a detached voice, nodding towards

the sitting-room: 'You've done a good deal of harm in there.'

Julia opened her eyes, and looked up with a stupid expression.

Miss Wyatt said: 'I don't think you'd better stay here any longer, do you? Come along now, here's your hat. You'd better go home and try to rest.'

Julia took the hat, looked at it with a surprised expression, then put it on awkwardly. She took out her powder and then returned it to her bag, obviously under the impression that she had used it. Miss Wyatt watched her with raised eyebrows. Then, as Julia still made no movement to get up, she put her hand on the other's shoulder and repeated firmly: 'Come along now, you must go. I can't have Norah upset any more. She's been through enough.'

'But I've been through something too,' said Julia in a sad, quiet voice. 'Don't you believe otherwise.'

'I daresay,' agreed Miss Wyatt. 'You can write to Norah if you've anything more to say, but you really must not stay here now.'

Julia got up. 'Oh, you needn't worry,' she said. 'I shall never bother any of you any more after this. Really.'

She walked towards the front door with a rather grotesque attempt at dignity. Then she stopped again.

'Come along now,' said Miss Wyatt soothingly but with finality. She put her hand on Julia's shoulder, gave her a very slight push, and shut the door on her gently.

7

Norah was sitting up on the sofa. She said: 'Where's Julia?'

'She's gone home,' answered Miss Wyatt. 'Much better for her.'

'Oh, no,' said Norah in a hysterical voice. 'We can't send her away like that. I don't believe she's got any money.'

'My dear,' said Miss Wyatt, 'just you lie down and keep youself still. Your sister's going to write.'

'Oh,' said Norah.

'O. course,' said Miss Wyatt with contempt. 'She'll write.'

Norah lay back, with her eyes shut. She thought: 'My God, how hard I've got!' Her lips trembled. 'What's happened to me?' For a moment she was afraid of herself.

Presently she heard from the kitchen the rattling noise of teacups in saucers. A feeling of rest crept from her knees upwards to her eyes. The clock ticked: 'You're young yet – young yet – young yet.'

Coming out of the chemist's shop at the end of the street Uncle Griffiths saw Julia approaching. As she walked she jerked herself from side to side, in the manner of a woman who is tired and no longer young walking on very high heels. People turned round to look at her.

Uncle Griffiths thought: 'Now what'll become of her, I wonder?' And, with decision, he crossed over to the other side of the street.

10. Notting Hill

As she walked, Julia felt peaceful and purified, as though she were a child. Because she could not imagine a future, time stood still. And, as if she were a child, everything that she saw was of profound interest and had the power to distract and please her. She looked into the faces of the people passing, not suspiciously or timidly, as was usual with her, but with a gentle and confident expression.

She went into the Tube station at the end of the road and took a ticket to Notting Hill Gate. As she sat waiting, a man hurried on to the platform, looked to the right and the left for a train, and then sat down heavily by her side. He was short and fat, dressed neatly in a grey suit, a dark overcoat, and a grey felt hat. He said, leaning towards Julia: 'Can you tell me, madam, if this platform is right for Oxford Circus?'

'Yes,' said Julia, 'I think so.'

'I'm a stranger here,' said the man. 'I don't know my way about very well.'

When the train came in he followed her into a carriage which was nearly empty. There were two men with their eyes fixed upon their newspapers, and a woman with a large attaché case who, when she saw that Julia was looking at her, drew down her lips with a prim and furtive expression.

The fat man, who had seated himself next to Julia, was saying: 'It's a bit lonely here for a stranger.'

He glanced at her sideways as he spoke.

'Are you a Londoner?'

'No,' said Julia.

'Ah,' he said, 'I thought not. I thought you looked a bit as if you were a stranger too.'

He went on talking. He said he was from South Africa, that he had spent most of his holiday in Berlin, but that he had thought he wanted to have a look at London too before he went back. Then, as if intoxicated by this long monologue about himself, he ended with, 'Would you care to have dinner with me tonight?'

'No,' Julia said. 'I can't.'

'Tomorrow, then?'

She shook her head.

The man said, 'Will you write or telephone me at this address? I shall be here for another couple of weeks.'

He gave her a card, on which were his name and the address of a club. Without looking at it, Julia let it drop into her lap, and said, 'Yes,' smiling mechanically, and: 'Yes, of course. Yes.'

When the train stopped at Notting Hill Gate station she got up quickly, and the card fell from her lap on to the floor. The man stared after her, and reddened. Then he looked hastily about him. No one was watching. He picked the card up, brushed it, and put it back into his pocket, crossed his legs, and composed his countenance.

2

Julia turned the key in her door and sat down on the bed with her hands on her knees, staring in front of her with a rather puzzled expression. Then she sighed, took off her hat, and lay down, smoothing the hair away from her forehead with a regular and mechanical gesture. She was horribly tired, and it was good to lie down. But her fingertips tingled and the muscles at the back of her neck were tight. Her thoughts were confused and blurred. She was certain that if a stranger were suddenly to appear before her and ask in a sharp voice: 'What's your name?' she would not know what to answer.

At about seven o'clock the yellow-haired maid brought up a letter:

Dear Madam Martin,

I am so sorry, but I must postpone our dinner tonight. I have a very urgent business appointment which simply has to be kept. Please forgive me. And I do hope we shall meet again before you go back to Paris.

With kindest regards,
Yours sincerely,
George Horsfield.

When Julia opened her eyes again it was dark. The idea of staying alone in the dark room was horrible to her, and as she dressed she twice looked suddenly and fearfully over her shoulder.

3

The street was a dark tunnel between the high walls of the houses. Down at the far end she saw a man walking very quickly, moving his arms as he walked like a tall, thin bird flapping its wings. They drew level under a lamp-post.

'I'm awfully glad I caught you,' said Mr Horsfield in a rather embarrassed voice. 'You see, I managed to scratch my appointment after all.'

Then he said: 'I felt I had to come. I wanted to see you.'

'I'm glad,' said Julia, but without surprise. 'I didn't want to be alone this evening.'

'Good,' said Mr Horsfield heartily. 'And you can dine with me?'

She looked surprised at the question and nodded.

As they walked along side by side, Mr Horsfield felt that her simplicity was touching.

He said: 'D'you like the place we went to the other night? Shall we go back there?'

She muttered: 'I'm tired, too tired to go far. It must be somewhere quite near.'

'I don't know a decent place round here,' said Mr Horsfield.

'It doesn't matter,' she answered. 'Anywhere will do – anywhere near.'

'What is it? Is anything the matter?' Mr Horsfield inquired.

She wanted to laugh and say: 'You don't suppose I'm mad, do you? To tell you what's the matter. You'd simply make some excuse to go off and leave me if I told you what was really the matter.' As if at this time of day she did not know that when you were in trouble the only possible thing to do was to hide it as long as you could.

She said: 'Why, no. Nothing's the matter.'

'Well, there's an Italian place not far off. Shall we try it?'

4

The resturant was long and narrow. Red-shaded lamps stood on the tables, and the walls were decorated with paintings of dead lobsters and birds served up on plates ready to be eaten, with flowers and piles of fruit in gilt baskets.

When Julia and Mr Horsfield came in the atmosphere in the restaurant was tense. A row was going on. One of the customers was bawling at the waiter that the soup was muck, and the other diners were listening with shocked but rather smirking expressions, like good little boys who were going to hear the bad little boy told off. The complainant, who must have been sensitive and have felt the universal disapproval, put up his hand to shield a face that grew redder and redder. However, he bawled again: 'Take it away. I won't eat it. It's not mulligatawny, it's muck.'

Mr Horsfield said: 'Let's have a gin-and-vermouth and go somewhere else.'

'No,' said Julia. 'Why? It's quite all right here.'

The rebellious gentleman was handed a bill and walked out, his face crimson, but still stubborn. The waiter said loudly to his back: 'Some people don't know how to behave themselves in a good-class restaurant.' And a very thin woman, dressed in black, who was sitting at the cash-desk, echoed him in a thin, mincing voice: 'Some people aren't used to a good-class restaurant.'

The door swung violently behind the back of the rebellious gentleman and immediately an atmosphere of restraint, decorum, and perfect gentility reigned in the restaurant. Even the fat Italian seated opposite to Mr Horsfield was affected by it. He began to pick his teeth with a worried expression, shielding the toothpick with one hand.

All through the meal Mr Horsfield talked without thinking of what he was saying. He was full of an absurd feeling of expectancy.

He noticed that Julia appeared fatigued, as if she had been crying. Yet he thought, too, that her face was thinner and somehow more youthful than when he had last seen her. Her eyes had a vague expression when she looked at him, as though she did not see him.

Outside a fine rain was falling. The darkness was greasy in spite of the rain. A woman in a long macintosh passed them, muttering to herself and looking mournful and lost, like a dog without a master.

Julia said: 'What's that over there? That red light with "Dancing"? Let's go there.'

5

They went up a narrow flight of stairs into a large room where about a dozen people were sitting at small tables and drinking lemonade or coffee. A gramophone was playing *Hallelujah*, and two couples were dancing in a square space in the middle of the room. The girls were young and pretty. Of the two men, one was young, with sleek hair and a self-satisfied expression. The other male dancer was elderly, nearer seventy than sixty, thin, dressed in a very loosely fitting grey suit. His face was cadaverous, his nose long and drooping He smiled continually as he danced, displaying very yellow teeth.

Mr Horsfield looked round at this scene and sighed. He felt a slight astonishment. He had never before encountered a place like this in London. It was more to be expected in the provinces or in a very distant suburb.

He said to the hovering waiter: 'Two coffees, please.'

Julia was looking at the old man dancing with an absorbed expression. Mr Horsfield said: 'Will you have coffee?'

Julia shook her head and answered, without moving her eyes: 'No, thanks, a *fine* – a brandy.'

'I'm afraid it's too late,' he explained. 'But, you know, I think we'd be in time for a drink at the Café Royal.'

'But it's all right here, isn't it?'

The gramophone stopped. A woman appeared from a room at the back, and put another record on. The old gentleman and another man in plus fours began to dance again with different partners. Mr Horsfield perceived that the feeling of mellowness and good-nature induced by the Chianti at dinner was deserting him.

After a time he said to Julia: 'Don't you think it's a bit lugubrious here?'

He felt that he disliked the place and he was irritated by the monosyllabic answers Julia made whenever he spoke to her. It was as if she were hardly listening to what he was saying. He thought that she looked at the dancers as if she had never seen anybody dancing before.

When they had been sitting for about half an hour and he was about to say: 'Look here, do you mind going and trying somewhere else?' he saw that the old gentleman was approaching their table. He walked mincingly, on the tips of his toes.

'May I have the pleasure?' he said to Julia.

As he leaned over the table his face was all bones and hollows in the light of the lamp striking upwards, like a skeleton's face.

'Wonderful old chap!' thought Mr Horsfield. He looked across at Julia. Her eyes had a surprised, even horror-stricken expression.

'Yes, I'd like to,' she said in a breathless voice.

She got up. Her manner was constrained, full of an unnecessary bravado.

'She really is a bit odd,' thought Mr Horsfield. But he felt irritated and depressed. He would not let himself look at the dancers for a time.

When he did so, Julia was being hugged very tightly by her partner, who hung a little over her shoulder, pervading her, as it were, and smiling. How idiotic all this dancing was, idiotic and rather sinister!

Her body looked abandoned when she danced, but not voluptuously so. It was the abandonment of fatigue.

Mr Horsfield lowered his eyes moodily, so that as Julia and her partner passed his table he saw only her legs, appearing rather too plump in flesh-coloured stockings. She seemed to him to be moving stiffly and rather jerkily. It was like watching a clockwork toy that has nearly run down.

'I congratulate you on your partner, sir. I congratulate you on your partner,' the old fool was saying. Then he hung about talking, obviously waiting for the gramophone to start again.

Mr Horsfield smiled unwillingly, and said something polite. Then he said he wanted to get some cigarettes and left the room as they began to dance again. It took him some time to find an automatic machine.

When he got back to the place the red light outside the door was out. He looked at his watch. It was five minutes to twelve. He mounted the stairs very quickly.

Julia was sitting alone at the table. He raised his eyebrows and said in an ironical way: 'Well?'

She laughed so hysterically that he was taken aback, and glanced round rather nervously. The man in plus fours, who was staring at them, said something with a sneering expression on his face. 'The tick!' thought Mr Horsfield, staring coldly back. He signalled to the waiter.

'Come along, this place will be shutting now, I expect,' he said to Julia.

6

In the taxi she leaned her head back, and shut her eyes. He thought that he had never seen anyone stay so perfectly still.

When they stopped at her boarding-house, he put his hand on hers and said: 'Here we are.'

They got out, and he paid the driver.

'Good night,' said Mr Horsfield mechanically.

'No,' she whispered.

He stared at her.

She said: 'You mustn't leave me. Don't leave me. You must stay with me. Please.'

He thought: 'I knew she'd do this.'

Then he said in a slow voice: 'Of course I will, if you want me to.'

11. It Might Have Been Anywhere

She mounted the steps without a word, and put her latch-key into the door.

'But if anybody sees you?' she asked.

Her voice sounded as if she were shivering. He thought: 'Well, you'll get turned out, my girl, that's a sure thing.' He said: 'It looks to me as if everybody in here has gone to bed long ago. I can walk without making any noise. Nobody will hear me, I promise you. Do the stairs creak?'

'The top flight does a little,' she said. 'Not the others. My room's right at the top.'

'All right,' he said. 'I'll be careful. I can walk pretty quietly.'

He put his hand on her arm, and felt that she was shivering. This added to his sensation of excitement and triumph.

'Come along,' he said.

He turned the key and walked first into the house. ·

When the door shut behind them they were in darkness and silence.

They reached the staircase. He put his hand on the banisters, and mounted noiselessly after her. She was invisible in the darkness, but he followed the sound of her footsteps, placing his feet very carefully, so that they made no sound.

The stairs were solid; there was not a creak.

They mounted silently, like people in a dream. And as in a dream he knew that the whole house was solid, with huge rooms – dark, square rooms, crammed with unwieldy furniture covered with chintz; darkish curtains would hang over the long windows. He knew even the look of the street outside when the curtains were drawn apart – a grey street, with high, dark houses opposite.

On the landing of the fourth floor Julia stopped for a

moment and listened. Then they went together up the last flight of wooden stairs.

There were three doors on the landing. She opened one of them very cautiously, switched on a light, and turned the key on the inside when he had passed her.

It was a large room, sparsely furnished. Mr Horsfield walked over to the window, which looked out on to the common garden at the back shared by all the houses on that side of the street. A square of blackness. He saw the bare branches of a tree, like fine lace, against the blackness. He heard the throb and far-off, calling whistle of a train. He thought: 'That must be the Great Western.'

A little playful wind lifted the curtains.

'Do shut the window,' she said. 'It's cold.'

He shut the window and pulled the curtains across it, then turned back into the room. He tried to do this without making any noise at all.

'I've only got one neighbour,' she said. 'She's asleep. Listen. . . . And there's a bathroom. That's all.'

She sighed very deeply, bent down, and lighted the gas-fire.

'Sit there, I'll have this cushion.'

She leaned her head back, and said: 'I'm so tired, so tired.'

He stretched out his hand to touch her hair, and then drew it back because something sensitive in him was puzzled and vaguely unhappy.

He said: 'Well, your partner was a good show, don't you think?'

'No,' she said. 'No, I thought him horrible, horrible.'

'Then why did you dance with him?'

'Sometimes one has to do things, haven't you ever felt that? You're very lucky, then. But if you haven't felt it, it's no use talking. Because you won't believe.'

'Don't you be so sure,' he said, 'about what I've felt and what I haven't felt.'

She said: 'D'you know what I think? I think people do what they have to do, and then the time comes when they can't any more, and they crack up. And that's that.'

'Yes,' he said, 'and perhaps I know something about cracking up too. I went through the war, you know.'

'I was twenty when the war started,' she told him. 'I rather liked the air raids.'

He began to stroke her hair mechanically. He pushed it upwards from the nape of her neck. He had imagined that her hair would be harsh to the touch, because he was certain that she dyed it, and dyed hair was always harsh to the touch. But in pushing it upwards it felt soft and warm, like the feathers of a very small bird. He stroked it first with the palm of his hand, and then with the back, and felt an extraordinary pleasure.

She said: 'You're awfully good to me.'

'You mustn't say that,' said Mr Horsfield, pulling his hand away abruptly. 'I absolutely forbid you to say that. I mean, it's the most fearful rot to say it.'

She said: 'No, you're good and kind and dear to me.'

He leaned forward and stared at her, and she looked back at him in a heavy, bewildered, sleepy way.

'She asked me up here,' he thought. 'She asked me.'

When he kissed her, her body was soft and unresisting.

There was a subdued rumble of trains in the distance. He thought again: 'The Great Western.'

You are thirsty, dried up with thirst, and yet you don't know it until somebody holds up water to your mouth and says: 'You're thirsty, drink.' It's like that. You are thirsty, and you drink.

And then you wonder all sorts of things, discontentedly and disconnectedly.

'But the worst of it is,' he thought, 'that one can never know what the woman is really feeling.'

2

He moved cautiously, and at once she opened her eyes.

'What is it?' she asked. 'You aren't going? You promised to stay with me.'

He was astonished at the sharpness in her voice. He said: 'My dear, of course. I'll lie on these two cushions by the side of your bed. I just thought you'd sleep better like that.'

He got the cushions and lay down, wondering what the time was. He thought: 'I wonder if they get up early here.'

Her arm was hanging down by the side of the bed. It looked pathetic, like a child's arm. He said: 'Julia, your hand is so lovely it makes me want to cry.'

'Oh,' she said, 'I was awfully pretty when I was a kid. Really I was, *sans blague*.'

'Don't talk like that,' said Mr Horsfield in a gruff voice. 'Of course you're pretty now.'

She sighed and turned over. Neither of them spoke again, and the next time he looked at her she seemed to be sleeping. He lit a cigarette and smoked it very slowly. Then he looked at her again with a rather stealthy expression, got up, and tiptoed to the window and pulled the curtains aside.

He looked out. A freshness came up from the garden. It was light enough to see the leaning trees and the bare brown patches of earth trodden by the feet of children playing. He thought: 'It's getting light. I must clear out.'

He looked at his watch. It was five o'clock. Again he gave a cautious glance at the bed. Then he tore a leaf out of his note-book and wrote:

Dear,

It's morning. So I'm going, or I'll risk meeting somebody on the stairs. I don't want to wake you. You might not get off to sleep again, and you look tired. I kiss your lovely hands and your lovely dark eyelids (what is the stuff you put on them?).

He stopped, frowned, pressed his lips together and tapped the pencil against his finger-nail. Then he went on writing:

I'll be here about six tomorrow evening or earlier if I can manage it. You are adorable.

Good-bye,
G.H.

He folded the sheet, addressed it, and put the note on the mantelpiece in a prominent position.

Every moment his desire to get out of the room was growing stronger. He tiptoed to the door, carrying his shoes in his hand, opened and shut it with infinite precaution, and crept down the still-dark stairs as silently as he could.

In the dimness of the hall a white face glimmered at him. He started, and braced himself for an encounter. Then, relieved, he saw it was a bust of the Duke of Wellington. He put his shoes on hastily and fumbled his way to the front-door.

3

When the door closed behind him he felt an extraordinary relief. At once the whole affair took on a normal and slightly humorous aspect. He smiled as he bent down to tie his shoelaces.

When he lifted his head he saw a policeman, who was standing on the pavement a few paces away, staring disapprovingly at him. The policeman stood with his legs very wide apart and his mouth pursed, looking extremely suspicious.

'This is grotesque,' muttered Mr Horsfield. He did not know whether he meant the policeman, or his excess of caution, or the Duke of Wellington, or the night he had just spent.

The two men stared at each other for a few seconds. Then Mr Horsfield said: 'Good morning, constable.'

'Perhaps I ought to have said sergeant,' flashed across his mind, for at the moment he was in dread of the policeman.

The policeman did not answer, but he slowly turned his head as Mr Horsfield passed and watched him as he walked quickly along the street in the direction of Ladbroke Grove.

12. Childhood

Every day is a new day. Every day you are a new person.

Julia felt well and rested, not unhappy, but her mind was strangely empty. It was an empty room, through which vague memories stalked like giants.

She read Mr Horsfield's note, and it was as if she were reading something written by a stranger to someone she had never seen.

She lay down stiff and straight on her back, with her arms close to her side. Every day is a new day; every day you are a new person. What have you to do with the day before?

There was a sharp rap at the door and she started violently. Her heart jumped in her side and hurt her.

The maid came in without waiting for an answer to her knock and asked: 'Have you finished with the breakfast tray?'

Keeping her eyes shut, Julia said: 'Yes, I've quite finished.'

'I'm supposed to get the bedrooms done by twelve,' said the girl.

'Will you leave mine this morning?' said Julia. 'I'll do it myself.' She would have liked to put her head under the sheets to escape from the girl's cold, pale blue stare. Or to get up and push her out of the room and curse her and bang the door after her.

'Well, I'm supposed to get the rooms done in the morning,' the girl repeated in a monotonous voice as she went out.

Julia leant over, took a small glass from the dressing-table and looked at herself. She looked at her hand, too, with the unaccustomed ring on it. It was rather tight, because her mother's hand had been so small and slim.

She wondered why the maid had looked at her with such unfriendly eyes. But hadn't she always suspected,

ever since she knew anything, that human beings were –
for no reason or for any reason – unfriendly?

When you were a child, you put your hand on the trunk
of a tree and you were comforted, because you knew that
the tree was alive – you felt its life when you touched it –
and you knew that it was friendly to you, or, at least, not
hostile. But of people you were always a little afraid.

When you are a child you are yourself and you know
and see everything prophetically. And then suddenly
something happens and you stop being yourself; you become what others force you to be. You lose your wisdom
and your soul.

How far back could you remember?

The last time you were really happy – happy about
nothing? When you were happy about nothing you had
to jump up and down. 'Can't you keep still, child, for
one moment?' No, of course you couldn't keep still. You
were too happy, bursting with happiness. You ran as if you
were flying, without feeling your feet. And all the time
you ran, you were thinking, with a tight feeling in your
throat: 'I'm happy – happy – happy . . . '

That was the last time you were really happy about
nothing, and you remembered it perfectly well. How old
were you? Ten? Eleven? Younger . . . yes, probably
younger.

And you could remember the first time you were afraid.

You were walking along a long path, shadowed for
some distance by trees. But at the end of the path was an
open space and the glare of white sunlight. You were
catching butterflies. You caught them by waiting until
they settled, and then creeping up silently on tiptoe and
squatting near them. Then, when they closed their wings,
looking like a one-petalled flower, you grabbed them
quickly, taking hold low down or the wings would break
in your hand.

When you had caught the butterfly you put it away in
an empty tobacco tin, which you had ready. And then you

walked along, holding the tin to your ear and listening to the sound of the beating of wings against it. It was a very fascinating sound. You wouldn't have thought a butterfly could make such a row.

Besides, it was a fine thing to get your hand on something that a minute before had been flying around in the sun. Of course, what always happened was that it broke its wings; or else it would fray them so badly that by the time you had got it home and opened the box and hauled it out as carefully as you could it was so battered that you lost all interest in it. Sometimes it was too badly hurt to be able to fly properly.

'You're a cruel, horrid child, and I'm surprised at you.'

And, of course, you simply did not answer this. Because you knew that what you had hoped had been to keep the butterfly in a comfortable cardboard-box and to give it the things it liked to eat. And if the idiot broke its own wings, that wasn't your fault, and the only thing to do was to chuck it away and try again. If people didn't understand that, you couldn't help it.

That was the first time you were afraid of nothing – that day when you were catching butterflies – when you had reached the patch of sunlight. You were not afraid in the shadow, but you were afraid in the sun.

The sunlight was still, desolate, and arid. And you knew that something huge was just behind you. You ran. You fell and cut your knee. You got up and ran again, panting, your heart thumping, much too frightened to cry.

But when you got home you cried. You cried for a long time; and you never told anybody why.

The last time you were happy about nothing; the first time you were afraid about nothing. Which came first?

2

'What have you done all day?' said Mr Horsfield at dinner.

'Nothing. I just stayed in my room.'

Mr Horsfield said, shocked: 'What? Didn't you have

anything to eat? Well, eat now, for goodness' sake.'

'At about four o'clock,' she said, 'I went in next door and the woman there gave me a cup of tea.'

'Do you mean the one that was snoring?'

'Yes.'

'Why ever did you go in there?'

'I don't know. I didn't want to be alone, I suppose.'

'Haven't you been doing anything? Have you been just lying there and thinking?'

She made no answer.

He asked, with a certain curiosity: 'What do you think about, Julia?'

She said: 'All the time about when I was a kid.'

'It's the easiest thing in the world to imagine you a kid.' Mr Horsfield felt sentimental about her. And then he wanted to laugh at himself because he was feeling sentimental.

She said she wanted to go to a cinema. She did not like plays; she had got out of the way of plays. They seemed unreal.

3

In the taxi he said to her: 'Do you know what you've done for me, Julia? You've given me back my youth. That's a big thing to do for anybody, isn't it?'

He went on: 'Look here, I can't take you back to my house tonight, because I've got a friend staying there. And a hotel would be perfectly foul. Do you mind if I come up to your room again?'

'Oh, no, I don't mind,' she said. 'I don't mind at all. Why should I mind?'

13. The Staircase

'You go first, and I'll follow you, like last night.'

He heard a rustling sound, the noise of Julia's dress, which was of stiff silk.

On the third landing she stopped. He knew it, because he could not hear the sound of her dress any longer. He heard her breathing loudly, as though she were exhausted. After a few seconds he whispered: 'Julia.'

She did not answer.

'Oh Lord,' he thought, 'What's the matter now?'

He waited a little longer, wondering whether he ought to strike a match, then walked carefully forwards, and passed her, groping for the banisters. His foot struck the first stair of the next flight, and he was convinced that he had made a very loud noise; yet somehow he did not wish to strike a match or speak again.

He groped and touched her hand, then her arm, and the fur collar of her coat. Then he ran his fingers downwards again, as a blind man might have done. He felt a strange pleasure in touching her like that – wordlessly, in the dark.

She said in a loud voice: 'Oh God, who touched me?'

He was too much astonished to answer.

'Who touched me?' she screamed. 'Who's that? Who touched my hand? What's that?'

'Julia!' he said.

But she went on screaming loudly: 'Who's that? Who's that? Who touched my hand?'

'Well,' thought Mr Horsfield, 'that's torn it.' He wondered if he would have time to bolt; dismissed the idea. There must be an electric switch somewhere.

He got his hand on to the wall, and began to feel for it. Matches. . . .

He said: 'Julia, my dear . . . '

Then the lights on the landing went on, and two bedroom doors opened simultaneously. Out of one appeared a dark young man with tousled hair, wearing striped pyjamas. He gave one look; then, without a word or a change of expression, he went back into his room and slammed the door. Out of the second door emerged a lady in a pink dressing-gown, with her hair hidden by a slumber-net. She was a young and good-looking woman, and she advanced upon Mr Horsfield with an air of authority. She was certainly the lady of the house.

'I'm frightfully sorry,' he said. His lips stretched themselves of their own accord into a conventional and very apologetic smile. 'Madame Martin isn't very well.'

The lady stared at Julia. In spite of himself, Mr Horsfield also turned and stared at Julia as though he had never seen her before. She made a movement of her mouth which was like a grimace. Then she said: 'I'm sorry. I'm not well. The stairs are so dark. I thought somebody touched me and I was frightened. I'm sorry if I disturbed you.'

The lady advanced two steps. Something in the way she walked and the poise of her head reminded Mr Horsfield of a cat advancing upon a mouse. She said in a soft, smooth voice: 'Well, I'm sorry you're ill, Mrs Martin. But you need not be frightened, you know. There are no dark corners in my house. I don't allow dark corners in my house.'

'Oh, nonsense,' said Mr Horsfield. 'Your stairs are dark enough, anyhow.' He added, in rather a high voice: 'After all, it's only just after twelve.'

Someone called up from the floor below: 'What's the matter, Mrs Atherton?'

'Nothing,' said the lady, peering over the banisters, 'nothing at all.'

A feeling which was a reaction against her pleasant voice, her pink dressing-gown, and the net over her hair swept over Mr Horsfield. He put his arm round Julia, and said: 'Come along, my dear.'

He knew that he looked a fool, but he did not care.

'Who was it touched me?' said Julia. Her eyes were

very wide open, the pupils dwindled to pin-points.

'But, my dear,' he said, 'I touched you.'

She shook her head.

'You were behind me.'

'Yes, but I passed you on the landing.'

'I thought it was – someone dead,' she muttered, 'catching hold of my hand.'

'Oh, Julia, my dear, look here, you're sick. Let me help you.'

The strangest understandings, the wildest plans, lit up his brain – together with an overwhelming contempt for the organization of society. Someone knocked at the door. Mrs Atherton, still wearing her pink dressing-gown but without the slumber-net, was there. She said: 'I came to see if there is anything I can do.'

'No, thank you,' said Julia. 'Nothing.'

'Ah,' said Mrs Atherton. She gazed at some point beyond both Julia and Mr Horsfield, looking utterly sure of herself.

'Are you all right?' said Mr Horsfield in an undecided voice.

Mrs Atherton waited.

'Damn and blast this landlady,' thought Mr Horsfield. He was opening his mouth to say: 'Look here, get out,' when Julia said: 'Good night.'

He looked at her.

'I'm all right,' she said.

Her eyes were cold and hostile. 'As if she hates me,' he thought.

He knew that she wanted nothing but to be left alone and to sleep.

She was very tired, her muscles were relaxed, her eyes half shut. She was thinking: 'Nothing matters. Nothing can be worse than how I feel now, nothing.' It was like a clock ticking in her head, 'Nothing matters, nothing matters. . . . '

'Good night,' she said again, in a cold withdrawn voice.

Mr Horsfield still hesitated.

'I'll call at ten o'clock tomorrow morning,' he said.

Mrs Atherton was still waiting. When he went out she followed him, without having once looked directly at Julia.

2

Mr Horsfield decided that he would walk home. He would try to walk off this feeling of rage and disappointment.

As he walked he began to plan what he would do the next morning. He imagined himself going into Julia's bedroom and talking, telling everything that was in his heart. He would hold her two hands and take her close to the window and say: 'Don't look at me like that. That was how you looked at me last night. Why should you look at me suspiciously, as if I were one of the others? I'm not one of the others; I'm on your side. Can't you see that? I'm for you and for people like you, and I'm against the others. Can't you see that?' he would say.

'I hate things as much as you do,' he would say. 'I'm just as fed up as you are. You hate hotly like a child because you've been hurt. But I hate coldly, and that's worse. I'm ready to chuck up everything and clear out. Lots of us are like that. Just the touch is wanted – something to set us off. You, and what happened last night, have done that for me.'

He stopped elaborating his speech to Julia. He thought: 'Anyhow I must clear out – get away. A succession of uncongenial tasks – that's what my life is. I'll chuck everything – sell the business for what it will fetch, get something out of life before I'm too old to feel. Get a bit of sun anyway.'

The sun. Oh, God, this stuffy, snuffy life! A white house with green blinds. . . .

He turned into the narrow street in which he lived. It was cobble-stoned and silent. There was a wall at the end, overhung by four stark trees.

His cat, waiting in his gateway, galloped to meet him as a dog might have done. It gave a soft, purring cry. Mr Horsfield bent down to stroke it, saying; 'Pretty Jones.'

The cat arched its back and purred again. In the light of the street-lamps its eyes shone, yellow-green, rather malevolent.

'Well, come on in then,' said Mr Horsfield. 'Come on in. And do get out of my way.'

There was nobody in the sitting-room. He got himself a whisky and soda and sat down. He realized that he was very tired.

Two walls of the room were covered with books almost from the ceiling to the floor. It was a low-pitched room, and there was only one small window. Nevertheless, it had a pleasant and peaceful, even spacious, appearance.

He thought: 'I don't see how I can bring her here exactly. . . . I can't possibly bring her here.'

Suddenly he saw Julia not as a representative of the insulted and injured, but as a solid human being. She must be taken somewhere – not later than the next morning. She must have a bed to sleep in, food, clothes, companionship – or she would be lonely; understanding of her own peculiar point of view – or she would be aggrieved.

He saw all this with great clarity, and felt appalled.

But he must find a room for her. He would have to. In Paddington or obscurer Bloomsbury.

Undertaking a fresh responsibility was not the way to escape when you came to think of it. . . .

He suddenly remembered that, after all, he was not in love with Julia; and he thought; 'I am not going to be rushed into anything.'

14. Departure

Julia was packing her trunk when Mr Horsfield arrived the next morning. He asked whether the landlady had told her to go.

'She told me that a woman who always stays here had written to ask when the room would be vacant. Would I prefer to leave this morning or this afternoon? So I said this morning.'

'Don't worry,' he said. 'Don't worry. I'll find a place for you.'

But he was shocked to see how old she looked. She had made herself up badly; that must be it. A faint revulsion mingled with his feeling of disappointment. He could not help thinking: 'Oh Lord, where is this going to lead me? Where is this going to stop?'

Then she said: 'I'm going back to Paris.' And he felt relieved. He said in a perfunctory voice: 'But why? Why not stay here?'

She looked at him, and then looked away again quickly.

'I'll be able to manage better there, I think.'

'I see.' He was suddenly light-hearted, irresponsible, almost happy.

He began to think about money, and that he must raise something. He must give her all he could. He wondered how his balance stood at the bank.

He said: 'Look here, I'll come over soon and see you.'

'Yes, of course.' She stared at him, not sadly, but with a heavy, dead indifference.

She knelt down by her trunk and locked it. Then, still kneeling, she looked up and said: 'All right. Everything's ready.'

He felt a pain, deep down. Like the pain of a loss.

'Your bill?' he said.

'I've paid it. Everything's ready; everything's done. If you'll just call a taxi.'

She stood at the glass straightening her hat. Her face looked hard and sullen. She made an involuntary little grimace at herself and again Mr Horsfield felt that tugging pain, as of a disappointed child.

'Come on,' she said impatiently. 'You'll have to help with the trunk, for I don't believe the servants here will do it.'

She looked at him with an air of bravado, raising her shoulders slightly, and he said, without meaning to say it: 'You've got some pluck.'

As he went downstairs to find the taxi, he thought: 'It isn't the first time she's been turned out of a room, that's clear.'

2

Everything that he had imagined the night before seemed fantastic – fantastic as a fairy tale. Yet he still kept on thinking out plans, worrying over details. 'How would I do it if I were going to do it?'

He said: 'What about letters? Would you like to have letters forwarded to my address?'

Julia answered that the letter she was expecting had been sent to her that morning by messenger and that she did not think there would be any more.

He said, hesitatingly: 'About money. . . . '

She took an envelope out of her bag and handed it to him. 'Read that.'

The letter was written in a large, clear handwriting, rather like a boy's.

Dear Julietta,

I ought to have sent this before. I didn't forget, but I mislaid that address you gave me. I've thought a good deal over what you said to me and I am very sorry that things haven't gone well with you. I am sending you some money because I want you to have a rest and a holiday, but I am afraid that after this I can do no more.

Mr Horsfield did not know what to say; he wondered what he could say. So much depended on the amount Julia's friend had sent.

'He sent twenty quid,' she said in a matter-of-fact voice. 'So, you see, I'm quite all right. I don't want any more money.'

'Well, twenty quid won't last for ever.'

'He collects pictures, this man. I suppose he must have been always fond of pictures, but I didn't know that. I didn't know anything about him, really. You see, he never used to talk to me much. I was for sleeping with – not for talking to. And quite right, too, I suppose. My God, isn't life funny, though?'

She began to laugh.

'Of course, I didn't think about it like that at the time. It never dawned on me. He was a sort of god to me and everything he did was right. Isn't one a fool when one's a kid? But sometimes I used to pray that he'd lose all his money, because I imagined that if that happened I'd see him oftener. And then I'd imagine myself working for him, or somehow getting money to give him. He'd have thanked me if he'd known what I was praying for, wouldn't he?'

'Oh, I daresay he'd have felt flattered,' said Mr Horsfield.

The bottle of wine was empty; Julia had drunk most of it. He called the waiter and ordered another.

She said: 'Oh, but that was nothing to a girl I knew, who used to pray that the man she loved might go blind.'

'Good God, that was surely a bit excessive, wasn't it?'

'Yes; so that he might be entirely dependent on her, d'you see? She loved him awfully and he made her jealous. But I didn't pray that. Oh, no, I couldn't have prayed that. . . . But I did pray about the money. It's pretty funny, isn't it? "After this I can do no more." "Good-bye-ee. Don't cry-ee." Do you remember that?' she said.

'Yes, I remember.'

He was thinking: 'It's so easy, isn't it, to be as bloody to you as everybody else has been?'

He said: 'Look here, in a week or ten days I'll come over to see you. Or, if I can't manage that, I'll send you some money.'

His voice was cold, but he could not help it. He could not put any warmth into it.

Her face grew very red. He averted his eyes.

'I don't care whether you send me any money or not,' she said. 'And I don't care whether you come or not. Now then!'

A muscle under her left eye was twitching.

'If you think,' she said, 'that I care. . . . I can always get somebody, you see. I've known that ever since I've known anything.'

'I daresay,' said Mr Horsfield. He felt horrified by the loudness of her voice. He was sure that the people in the restaurant were beginning to stare at them.

'Yes,' she went on, even more loudly, 'I can. Don't you worry.'

Then her lips trembled, tears came into her eyes. She said: 'Hell to all of you! Hell to the lot of you . . . '

Something in Mr Horsfield's expression penetrated to her consciousness and she began to make grimaces in an effort to restrain herself.

He looked away from her.

She said sullenly: 'I'm sorry. You see, that's how I am.'

'Oh, that's all right.'

For the life of him he was unable to think of anything more sympathetic; yet he could imagine everything she had left unsaid. He understood her, but in a cold and theoretical way.

He looked at his watch and saw with relief that it was nearly time to go.

3

On his way home Mr Horsfield tried to put Julia entirely
out of his mind.

As he was opening the door of his house he thought:
'Well, that's all over, anyway.' And then he wondered
how he should send money to her if she did not write. 'But,
of course, she will write,' he told himself.

He shut the door and sighed. It was as if he had altogether shut out the thought of Julia. The atmosphere of
his house enveloped him – quiet and not without dignity,
part of a world of lowered voices, and of passions, like
Japanese dwarf trees, suppressed for many generations.
A familiar world.

Part Three

1. Île de la Cité

The visit to London had lasted ten days, and already it was a little blurred in Julia's memory. It had become a disconnected episode to be placed with all the other disconnected episodes which made up her life.

Her hotel looked out on a square in the Île de la Cité, where the trees were formally shaped, much like the trees of a box of toys you can buy at Woolworth's. The houses opposite had long rows of windows, and it seemed to Julia that at each window a woman sat staring mournfully, like a prisoner, straight into her bedroom.

At night she slept heavily, without dreaming. When she awoke she was still weighed down with fatigue, so that she could dress only very slowly, and with great effort.

She thought: 'I've been back a week and three days – a week and four days today. Well, I can't go on like this.'

She got up and shut the window, so as not to be overlooked.

She wrote:

Jeune dame (36), conaissant anglais, français, allemand, cherche situation dame de compagnie ou gouvernante. Hautes références. . . .

As she wrote *références*, she thought: 'Now, where did I put that letter?' It had been given her three years before by a Frenchwoman.

A feeling of panic seized her. She was sure she had lost it. And if she had, where was she to get anything else that would serve as a reference? Her hands trembled with fright as she searched.

'Anything puts me in a state now,' she thought.

She found it at last, in an envelope with a card on which was written: '*Wien, le 24 août, 1920. Menu.*' At the back of it were a number of signatures.

She looked at the menu for a long time. 'I can't believe that was me.' And then she thought: 'No, I can't believe that this is me, now.'

She had worn a white crêpe de Chine dress, and red slippers.

'Of course, you clung on because you were obstinate. You clung on because people tried to shove you off, despised you, and were rude to you. So you clung on. Left quite alone, you would have let go of your own accord. The *Figaro* for the advertisement, of course.'

There was a knock at the door, and a postman came in with a registered letter. It was from Mr Horsfield.

My dear Julia,

I was awfully glad to get your card. I wish I could send you something more than the enclosed but, as you may have gathered times are a bit hard with me.

I'm afraid I shan't be able to turn up quite so soon as I had hoped, but if and when I can manage it I do hope you'll let me come to see you. You were a dear to me, and I feel most awfully grateful.

Wishing you the very best of luck,

Yrs.,
G.H.

Enclosed were two five-pound notes.

2

As soon as she got out-of-doors she felt calmer and happier. She told herself that, of course, it was the room which depressed her because it was so narrow, and because it was so horrible not to be able to open the window without having several pairs of eyes glued upon you. She thought: 'We're like mites in a cheese in that damned hotel.'

It was a very sunny day. The sun was as strong as if it were already summer.

She sat on one of the stone seats near the statue of Henri IV on the Pont Neuf.

An old woman mounted the steps leading from the *quais*. She had a white face, white frizzy hair, and a very pale blue apron. In the sun she looked transparent, like a ghost.

As Julia walked along the Quai des Orfèvres the light was silver and the wind was soft. The river was brown and green – olive-green under the bridges – and a rainbow coloured scum floated at the sides. Anything might happen. Happiness. A course of face massage.

She began to imagine herself in a new black dress and a little black hat with a veil that just shadowed her eyes. After all, why give up hope when so many people had loved her? . . . 'My darling. . . . My lovely girl. . . . *Mon amour*. . . . *Mon petit amour* . . .'

But when the men who passed glanced at her, she looked away with a contracted face. Something in her was cringing and broken, but she would not acknowledge it.

In her mind she was repeating over and over again, like a charm: 'I'll have a black dress and hat and very dark grey stockings.'

Then she thought: 'I'll get a pair of new shoes from that place in the Avenue de l'Opéra. The last ones I got there brought me luck. I'll spend the whole lot I had this morning. It seems a mad thing to do, but I don't care. . . . Besides, getting that job is all bluff. What chance have I really?'

A ring with a green stone for the forefinger of her right hand.

At lunch she drank a half-bottle of Burgundy and felt very hopeful. She spent the whole afternoon in the Galeries Lafayette choosing a dress and a hat. Then she went back to her hotel, dressed herself in her new clothes, and walked up and down her room, smoking. She decided that after dinner she would go to Montparnasse. She would go latish – between ten and eleven.

At seven o'clock a gramophone started in a little café

near by. Simultaneously, a smell of sulphur which had been perceptible for the last hour suddenly grew so strong that it was almost impossible to breathe. Curls of acrid smoke came in under the bottom of the door.

There was a knock, and the landlady came in to explain that the gentleman who had occupied the next room had left a few lice behind him and, as they were clean people, they had been obliged to take precautions. She said: 'I thought there wasn't anybody in on this floor. Would you like to come down and sit in the bureau?'

Julia said no, that she was going out.

3

When she had finished dinner it was nearly nine o'clock. She walked in the direction of the river. It fascinated her, because every hundred yards or so it was different. Sometimes it was sluggish and oily, then, after you had walked a little farther, the current flowed very strongly.

She watched the shadows of the branches trembling in the water. In mid-stream there was a pool of silver light where the shadows danced and beckoned. She thought: 'It can't be the trees right out there.'

A cloud of smoke was coming from the funnel of a flat boat. Shadows of smoke in the water.

She leaned against the wall, and watched the shadows as they danced, but without joy. They danced, they twisted, they thrust out long, curved, snake-like arms and beckoned.

Someone behind her said: 'There's something that doesn't go, madame?'

She turned and saw a policeman just behind her. She answered in a cold voice: 'I haven't the slightest intention of committing suicide, I assure you.'

'Oh, that wasn't my idea either,' said the policeman politely. '*Seulement* . . .'

She looked again at the river, and then said: 'What are those shadows, do you see? There, right in the middle of the water.'

'It's a tree, the branch of a tree.'

Julia thought: 'That's what *you* say.'

'Of course,' said the policeman, who was an affable and rather good-looking young man. 'That big branch, do you see?'

The shadows seemed not to be on the surface, but to be struggling, wriggling upwards from the depths of the water.

She said to the policeman: 'I was only looking.'

She walked off along the quay, went into a café, and had a *fine*. It was a low-down place. She sat and stared at the woman behind the counter.

The woman behind the counter was beautiful. When she spoke to the customers, her voice was very soft and her eyes were big and dark. She was a slim woman with full, soft breasts.

Julia had a great longing to go up to the woman and talk to her. It was rum; some people did look like that – not cruel, but kind and soft. One in a million looked like that.

She sat thinking: 'If I could talk to her, if only I could go up and tell her all about myself and why I am unhappy, everything would be different afterwards.'

When she came out of the café she walked towards the Place St Michel, and as she reached it, it began to rain. Everybody rushed to the cafés for shelter.

'I mustn't get my clothes wet,' she thought.

Just opposite was a Pathéphone Salon. She went in, sat down on one of the swivel-chairs, bought several discs, and, without changing the register before her, set the thing in motion. A woman's voice, harsh and rather shrewish, began to sing in her ear.

All the time she listened she was thinking: 'After all, what have I done? I haven't done anything.'

She felt the hardness of the receiver pressed up against her ear. The voice sang the chorus of a sentimental and popular song. '*Pars, sans te retourner, pars.*' An unlucky song.

Songs about parting were always unlucky. That was a sure thing.

She put the receiver down hastily and looked up something else.

2. The Second Unknown

The rain had nearly stopped when Julia came out of the Pathéphone Salon, but she thought she felt a few drops still falling. The air was very sweet. It smelt of trees and grass.

She crossed the street and went into the big café opposite. It was very full of talking and gesticulating men. The few women who were there were unpretentious and rather subdued.

She ordered a brandy and a blotter. After what seemed an interminable time the waiter brought the brandy.

'And the blotter, please,' she said.

After another long interval the blotter appeared.

She felt that her nerves were exposed and raw.

'Thank you,' she said in a sarcastic voice. 'That's quickly done, isn't it?'

The waiter was a fat, dark, good-looking young man with a mop of frizzy black hair. He stared at her, shrugged, made with his arms a large gesture which expressed to perfection a not ill-natured indifference.

'And another brandy,' she called after him with a black look.

She had meant to write to Mr Horsfield, but when she took up the pen she made meaningless strokes on the paper. And then she began to draw faces – the sort of faces a child would draw, made up of four circles and a straight line.

'Well,' she thought suddenly, 'no use getting into a state.'

She wrote on the paper: '*Doucement, doucement.*'

When she had finished the second brandy her plan of spending the evening in Montparnasse had retreated into the background of her mind. She only wanted to walk somewhere straight ahead.

She turned her back on the Place St Michel and began to walk towards the Châtelet. Then she realized that a man was walking just behind her. He kept step with her; he cleared his throat; he was getting ready to speak.

The man drew level with her and they walked on side by side. She turned her head away and pressed her lips together. She wanted to say: 'Go away, you're annoying me,' but a ridiculous bashfulness kept her from doing so.

They walked on side by side – tense, like two animals.

Julia thought: 'I can't stand this. When we pass the next lamp-post I'm going to tell him to go off.'

When they reached the next lamp she turned and looked at him. He was young – a boy – wearing a cap, very pale and with very small, dark eyes set deeply in his head. He gave her a rapid glance.

'*Oh, la la,*' he said. '*Ah, non, alors.*'

He turned about and walked away.

'Well,' said Julia aloud, 'that's funny. The joke's on me this time.'

She began to laugh, and on the surface of her consciousness she was really amused. But as she walked on her knees felt suddenly weak, as if she had been struck a blow over the heart. The weakness crept upwards.

As she walked she saw nothing but the young man's little eyes, which had looked at her with such deadly and impartial criticism.

She thought again: 'That was really funny. The joke was on me that time.'

2

The Place du Châtelet was a nightmare. A pale moon, like a claw, looked down through the claw-like branches of dead trees.

She turned to the left and walked into a part of the city which was unknown to her. 'Somewhere near the Halles,' she thought. 'Of course, at the back of the Halles.'

She saw a thin man, so thin that he was like a clothed skeleton, drooping in a doorway. And the horses, standing like statues of patient misery. She felt no pity at all.

It used to be as if someone had put out a hand and touched her heart when she saw things like that, but now she felt nothing. Now she felt indifferent and cold, like a stone.

'I've gone too far,' she thought. She sat down on the terrace of a little café and had another brandy.

And it was funny to end like that – where most sensible people start, indifferent and without any pity at all. Just saying: 'It's nothing to do with me. I've got my own troubles. It's nothing to do with me.'

3. Last

'That's the worst of the hot weather,' Mr Mackenzie was thinking. 'Somehow it always brings these accursed nuisances out of their shells.'

He had been having a row with a dirty old man who had insisted on playing a mandoline into his ear; and the waiter whom he had called to his assistance had seemed very unwilling to do anything definite about it. But, by a display of firmness, Mr Mackenzie had won. The dirty man was shambling away, down-at-heel and dejected.

It was a little café in the Rue Dauphine. He had never been there before and was never likely to return to it. But he had felt tired and had thought that a drink would refresh him. He sipped at it and stretched his legs and felt gladly conscious of the beginnings of a sensation of restfulness.

He glanced about him. The mandoline-player had disappeared, but Julia Martin was advancing towards him.

Mr Mackenzie checked an impulse to put a hand up to shield his face. It was too late; she had seen him. She met his eyes and looked away. She passed within a yard of him, still looking away.

'Well,' thought Mr Mackenzie. A blank expression came over his face. Then he thought suddenly: 'Good God, what is the use of all this bad blood?'

She walked on slowly, aimlessly, holding her head down.

The romantic side of his nature asserted itself. He got up and followed her. She was standing on the edge of the pavement, waiting for an opportunity to cross the street. He touched her arm.

'Hullo, Julia.'

'Hullo,' she said, looking round.

'Well, how are things?'

'All right,' she said.

Mr Mackenzie smiled, displaying all his teeth. He wavered for a moment. Then he said: 'Come along and have a drink.'

'All right,' she said.

They sat down – inside the little café this time. 'I'm not a bad sort,' he was thinking. 'Who says that I'm a bad sort? I wish all the swine who do could see me now. How many of them would give a drink to a woman who had smacked them in the face in public?'

'I'll have a Pernod, please,' said Julia.

She drank, and then cleared her throat. 'I've gone back to that hotel. You know – the one on the Quai Grands Augustins.'

'Oh, yes?' He did not know what she was talking about. 'Is it a good place?'

'Not bad. Only there's a woman upstairs who gives me a *cafard* – you know, who depresses me.'

'That's a bore for you,' said Mr Mackenzie.

She looked untidy. There were black specks in the corners of her eyes. Women go phut quite suddenly, he thought. A feeling of melancholy crept over him.

He said: 'It's getting pretty hot. You ought to get away for a change. I'm off tomorrow.'

She made no answer, but she finished her Pernod quickly.

'Lend me a hundred francs, will you?' she said. 'Please.'

This shocked Mr Mackenzie. He flushed. He said: 'Good Lord, yes.'

He stripped two ten-franc notes off a bundle of small change and pushed the rest over to her. 'Have this, will you?' he said. 'There's a bit more than a hundred there, I think.'

Julia put the money into her bag without counting it.

Mr Mackenzie fidgeted. 'I'm afraid I must be getting along now. Will you have another drink before I go?'

'Yes, another Pernod, please,' she said. And then: 'So long.'

'Good-bye,' said Mr Mackenzie.

The street was cool and full of grey shadows. Lights were beginning to come out in the cafés. It was the hour between dog and wolf, as they say.

READ MORE IN PENGUIN

In every corner of the world, on every subject under the sun, Penguin represents quality and variety – the very best in publishing today.

For complete information about books available from Penguin – including Puffins, Penguin Classics and Arkana – and how to order them, write to us at the appropriate address below. Please note that for copyright reasons the selection of books varies from country to country.

In the United Kingdom: Please write to *Dept. JC, Penguin Books Ltd, FREEPOST, West Drayton, Middlesex UB7 OBR*

If you have any difficulty in obtaining a title, please send your order with the correct money, plus ten per cent for postage and packaging, to *PO Box No. 11, West Drayton, Middlesex UB7 OBR*

In the United States: Please write to *Penguin USA Inc., 375 Hudson Street, New York, NY 10014*

In Canada: Please write to *Penguin Books Canada Ltd, 10 Alcorn Avenue, Suite 300, Toronto, Ontario M4V 3B2*

In Australia: Please write to *Penguin Books Australia Ltd, 487 Maroondah Highway, Ringwood, Victoria 3134*

In New Zealand: Please write to *Penguin Books (NZ) Ltd,182–190 Wairau Road, Private Bag, Takapuna, Auckland 9*

In India: Please write to *Penguin Books India Pvt Ltd, 706 Eros Apartments, 56 Nehru Place, New Delhi 110 019*

In the Netherlands: Please write to *Penguin Books Netherlands B.V., Keizersgracht 231 NL–1016 DV Amsterdam*

In Germany: Please write to *Penguin Books Deutschland GmbH, Friedrichstrasse 10–12, W–6000 Frankfurt/Main 1*

In Spain: Please write to *Penguin Books S. A., C. San Bernardo 117–6° E–28015 Madrid*

In Italy: Please write to *Penguin Italia s.r.l., Via Felice Casati 20, I–20124 Milano*

In France: Please write to *Penguin France S. A., 17 rue Lejeune, F–31000 Toulouse*

In Japan: Please write to *Penguin Books Japan, Ishikiribashi Building, 2–5–4, Suido, Tokyo 112*

In Greece: Please write to *Penguin Hellas Ltd, Dimocritou 3, GR–106 71 Athens*

In South Africa: Please write to *Longman Penguin Southern Africa (Pty) Ltd, Private Bag X08, Bertsham 2013*

CLASSICS OF THE TWENTIETH CENTURY

The Outsider Albert Camus

Meursault leads an apparently unremarkable bachelor life in Algiers, until his involvement in a violent incident calls into question the fundamental values of society. 'The protagonist of *The Outsider* is undoubtedly the best achieved of all the central figures of the existential novel' – *Listener*

Dark as the Grave wherein my Friend is Laid Malcolm Lowry

A Dantesque descent into hell: into Lowry's infernal landscape of Mexico – the Mexico of his masterpiece, *Under the Volcano* – and into Lowry's own personal abyss, reverberating with mental terrors and spiritual chasms.

I'm Dying Laughing Christina Stead

A dazzling novel set in the 1930s and 1940s when fashionable Hollywood Marxism was under threat from the savage repression of McCarthyism. 'The Cassandra of the modern novel in English ... reading her seems like plunging into the mess of life itself' – Angela Carter

The Desert of Love François Mauriac

Two men, father and son, share a passion for the same woman – attractive, intelligent and proud, but an outcast from respectable society because of her position as a 'kept woman'. 'He writes with an intense, almost tempestuous force about the life of the emotions' – Olivia Manning

The Expelled and Other Novellas Samuel Beckett

Rich in verbal and situational humour, these four stories offer the reader a fascinating insight into Beckett's preoccupation with the helpless individual consciousness, a preoccupation which has remained constant throughout his work.

Chance Acquaintances and Julie de Carneilhan Colette

Two contrasting works in one volume. Colette's last full-length novel, *Julie de Carneilhan* was 'as close a reckoning with the elements of her second marriage as she ever allowed herself'. In *Chance Acquaintances*, Colette visits a health resort, accompanied only by her cat.

FOR THE BEST IN PAPERBACKS, LOOK FOR THE 🐧

CLASSICS OF THE TWENTIETH CENTURY

Petersburg Andrei Bely

'The most important, most influential and most perfectly realized Russian novel written in the twentieth century' (*The New York Times Book Review*), *Petersburg* is an exhilarating search for the identity of the city, presaging Joyce's search for Dublin in *Ulysses*.

The Miracle of the Rose Jean Genet

Within a squalid prison lies a world of total freedom, in which chains become garlands of flowers – and a condemned prisoner is discovered to have in his heart a rose of monstrous size and beauty. Of this profoundly shocking novel Sartre wrote: 'Genet holds the mirror up to us: we must look at it and see ourselves.'

Labyrinths Jorge Luis Borges

Seven parables, ten essays and twenty-three stories, including Borges's classic 'Tlön, Uqbar; Orbis Tertius', a new world where external objects are whatever each person wants, and 'Pierre Menard', the man who rewrote *Don Quixote* word for word without ever reading the original.

The Vatican Cellars André Gide

Admired by the Dadaists, denounced as nihilist, defended by its author as a satirical farce: five interlocking books explore a fantastic conspiracy to kidnap the Pope and place a Freemason on his throne. *The Vatican Cellars* teases and subverts as only the finest satire can.

The Rescue Joseph Conrad

'The air is thick with romance like a thunderous sky...' 'It matters not how often Mr Conrad tells the story of the man and the brig. Out of the million stories that life offers the novelist, this one is founded upon truth. And it is only Mr Conrad who is able to tell it us' – Virginia Woolf

Southern Mail/Night Flight Antoine de Saint-Exupéry

Both novels in this volume are concerned with the pilot's solitary struggle with the elements, his sensation of insignificance amid the stars' timelessness and the sky's immensity. Flying and writing were inextricably linked in the author's life and he brought a unique sense of dedication to both.

BY THE SAME AUTHOR

Quartet

The winter-wet streets of Montparnasse, *pernods* in smoke-filled cafés, cheap hotel rooms and Marya Zelli, trying to make something substantial of her life – to resist the unreality that surrounds her. Alone, her Polish husband in prison, she has been taken up by an English couple who slowly overwhelm her with their passions. The husband demands, the wife fosters. Marya is left – as always – to comfort herself.

Voyage In The Dark

A brief liaison with a kindly but unimaginative man leads Anna to abandon the theatre and drift into the demi-monde of 1914 London: red-plush dinners in private rooms 'up West'; ragtime, champagne and whisky back at the flat; these, and a discreet tinkle of sovereigns in the small hours pave the way to disaster . . .

Good Morning, Midnight

Back in Paris for 'a quiet, sane fortnight', Sasha Jensen has just been rescued by a friend from drinking herself to death in a Bloomsbury bed-sitter. Despite a transformation act, new clothes and blonde cendré hair dye, Sasha still feels 'not quite as good as new'. Streets, shops and bars vividly evoke her Paris past: feckless husband Enno, baby born dead, sundry humiliations in abject jobs . . .

One night, a gigolo mistakes Sasha for a rich woman – she still has her fur coat – and their subsequent liaison somehow distils the essence of all that has gone before.

BY THE SAME AUTHOR

Wide Sargasso Sea

The novel that re-established Jean Rhys as a major British writer. *Wide Sargasso Sea* is the story of Antoinette Cosway, the Creole heiress who became the first Mrs Rochester, the mad wife in Charlotte Brontë's *Jane Eyre*.

'An imaginative feat almost uncanny in its vivid intensity' – Francis Wyndham.

Sleep It Off Lady

Sixteen tales, uncannily and vividly drawn together like the fragments of a single life – childhood innocence destroyed under a louring Caribbean sky; youthful disenchantment with the London stage life of the 1910s; brief encounters in the brittle gaiety of a Parisian nightclub and in London during the Blitz; followed by the slow, inevitable descent into old age and loneliness; and after death, the return.

Tigers are Better-Looking

A collection of short stories, first published in 1939, which includes a selection from Jean Rhys's 1927 volume of Paris stories, *The Left Bank*, of which Ford Madox Ford wrote in the Preface: 'One likes, in short to be connected with something good, and Miss Rhys's work seems to me to be very good, so vivid, so extraordinarily distinguished by the rendering of passion, and so true, that I wish to be connected with it.'